P. M. Hubbard and The Murder Room

>>> This title is part of The Murder Room, our series dedicated to making available out-of-print or hard-to-find titles by classic crime writers.

Crime fiction has always held up a mirror to society. The Victorians were fascinated by sensational murder and the emerging science of detection; now we are obsessed with the forensic detail of violent death. And no other genre has so captivated and enthralled readers.

Vast troves of classic crime writing have for a long time been unavailable to all but the most dedicated frequenters of second-hand bookshops. The advent of digital publishing means that we are now able to bring you the backlists of a huge range of titles by classic and contemporary crime writers, some of which have been out of print for decades.

From the genteel amateur private eyes of the Golden Age and the femmes fatales of pulp fiction, to the morally ambiguous hard-boiled detectives of mid twentieth-century America and their descendants who walk our twenty-first century streets, The Murder Room has it all. >>>

The Murder Room
Where Criminal Minds Meet

themurderroom.com

T0352445

P. M. Hubbard (1910–1980)

Praised by critics for his clean prose style, characterization, and the strong sense of place in his novels, Philip Maitland Hubbard was born in Reading, in Berkshire and brought up in Guernsey, in the Channel Islands. He was educated at Oxford, where he won the Newdigate Prize for English verse in 1933. From 1934 until its disbandment in 1947 he served with the Indian Civil Service. On his return to England he worked for the British Council, eventually retiring to work as a freelance writer. He contributed to a number of publications, including *Punch*, and wrote 16 novels for adults as well as two children's books. He lived in Dorset and Scotland, and many of his novels draw on his interest in and knowledge of rural pursuits and folk religion.

The Whisper in the Glen

P. M. Hubbard

An Orion book

Copyright © Caroline Dumonteil, Owain Rhys Phillips and Maria
Marcela Appleby Gomez 1972, 2012

The right of P. M. Hubbard to be identified as the author of this work
has been asserted in accordance with the Copyright, Designs and Patents
Act 1988.

This edition published by
The Orion Publishing Group Ltd
Orion House
5 Upper St Martin's Lane
London WC2H 9EA

An Hachette UK company
A CIP catalogue record for this book is available from the British Library

ISBN 978 1 4719 0087 7

www.orionbooks.co.uk

I

Kate sat in the middle of the almost abandoned kitchen. She sat leaning slightly forward, with her elbows on the table. There was another chair pulled in on the other side of the table. The two chairs and the table were the only movable furniture left. Richard came and stood in the doorway, looking at her. She did not hear him come and did not see him. She was staring out of the window, and he was out of her line of vision. They were both tired. Moves were an exhausting business, quite apart from the mental uncertainties. In this case the mental uncertainties were considerable.

He said, 'Tired?' and she turned and looked at him. She knew that he had been watching her for a moment before he had spoken to her, and that now he felt guilty about it. They had been married thirteen years, and had great respect for each other's privacy. She knew, too, that her good looks survived the dirty overall and the smear of dust on her forehead, and she wondered whether, when he looked at her like that, privately, he saw her as other men saw her. But it was one of the questions you did not ask.

She smiled at him. 'Exhausted,' she said. 'Aren't you?'

He came in and pulled out the other chair and sat opposite her across the empty table. 'Pretty well,' he said. 'But the end's in sight.'

He looked, in fact, more tired than she did. He was quite a bit older, for one thing. Also, although they had shared the physical work, he carried almost the whole mental burden. The move was his idea. For the same reason, Kate was not going out of her way to feel sorry for him. She had demurred when he suggested it, listened to his arguments and agreed. Once she had agreed, she would have been ashamed to drag her feet. But she was not going to lie awake at night wondering if they were doing the right thing. He could if he liked, and she was fairly certain he had, but that was up to him. If it turned out to be a mistake, he would have to think again. The thing was presumably not irrevocable. She said, 'So long as you're not too tired to cope when you get there. You've still got the drive up.'

He did not like that. She had not meant to gall him, but she should have known. The one suggestion he was not prepared to listen to was that he might have bitten off more than he could chew, simply with the job. He said, 'I know that. But I'll take it slow, and I've got a couple of days when I get there.'

'Well, don't let Dr Fagan rush you.'

He saw now that her concern was genuine. His moments of touchiness never lasted. He smiled at her. 'I won't,' he said. 'But you'll have to drop the Llanabba joke, or you'll be making it up there. From what I saw of Haskell, I doubt if he's got his Evelyn Waugh at his finger-tips, and I'm damned sure his wife hasn't, but someone may. Anyway, it isn't really fair. The school's not derelict, by any means. Plenty of money, I should think. A bit cranky, but even that's fashionable in its way.'

'Oh yes,' she said, 'we're all Gordonstoun now. So long as they don't make you wear the kilt and climb mountains.'

'Don't worry. They won't. They know that.' He looked at her, a little worried. 'The place really is lovely, you know. I'll be interested to see your Highland blood stirring. You'll probably insist on being called Catriona before you've been there a month.'

She wanted to reassure him now. Even the suggestion of dragged feet appalled her. She sat back and smiled at him.

2

'I doubt it, but you never know. Let's have some coffee. We can still manage that, at least.'

'Can we? That's fine. You make it, and I'll go and gather up the last few bits.'

He heaved himself out of his chair and went out with determined sprightliness. Kate got up and took the coffee things out of the basket. Catriona, she thought. Catriona Macinnes, born in Bombay and never been north of Newcastle. She even looked Highland. That was where her looks came from, all aquiline nose and cheekbones, with the fair skin and dark hair and grey-blue eyes. But now she was Kate Wychett, English on the mother's side, married to one of the most English men she had ever met and still, after all these years, in reaction against the expatriate extravagances of her dead father. Oh well, she thought, it would be interesting, anyhow. As for her blood's stirring, she supposed it still could at thirty-two, but she doubted if a landscape could do it. She put the water on the stove in the small saucepan and went back to her chair.

Never since Julia, no stirring of the blood over anything, presumably because the blood was plain scared of being stirred. She had never been able to make up her mind whether it would have been better or worse if they had had other children. They could have, judging by the ease with which she had started and produced Julia. But she had been full young when she married, and they had agreed not for a few years. Full young, that was her father's phrasing. Just young, she had been, not yet twenty, and damn all Scots nonsense. She had left it all to Richard, who had obliged with his usual consideration and efficiency. Not cold-blooded, exactly, because there was nothing wrong with Richard as a husband. She had been a virgin when she married, but he, in a respectable, unexplained, middle-class sort of way, had not, and she had never had any reason to regret either fact. Then they had decided it was time to start, and started she had at the drop of a hat and to everybody's satisfaction. And then when Julia was three, and they were starting to think about a boy to go with her, she had died of measles. Measles of all things, one of those occasional appalling lapses of a medical efficiency everybody took for granted.

That had been the moment of decision, and they had fluffed it between them. She knew now that she had wanted another child straight away, as people said that if your dog was run over, you should go straight out and buy another puppy of the same breed. But she had never managed to say so, and Richard, all kindness and consideration, had assumed the opposite, and he was not a man to be taken off his guard. Then the emotional numbness had settled on her, with the sudden, second-wave unexpectedness of delayed shock, and after that she had left Richard's assumptions undisturbed. What he had wanted she did not know. He had been a perfectly good father while his paternity lasted, just as he was a perfectly good husband, but she could not see him yearning for offspring in his own right; and she herself had wanted nothing. Nothing, anyhow, as emotionally demanding as a child. They were happy in bed, as they were out of it, in a secure, low-keyed sort of way, but they were giving no more hostages to fortune, and now Richard was forty-seven and she was thirty-two. The question did not arise, but if it had, she would have said they had left it too late for that kind of adventure.

They were proportionately freer for this kind. Making coffee in a saucepan in a derelict kitchen, because the better stuff was already stored, and the rest, in a couple of days' time, would be on its way to Scotland. Free to let Richard go and teach in a school nobody much had heard of, because the colonial administration he had been trained for had died under him, and he was finding the second-rate administrative jobs open to him at home increasingly depressing. Free

4

to starve in a genteel sort of way on a part-pension if he found he could not teach, even by the standards of Glenaidon, and he was by then too old to get back into administration. But she was not really worried. It was Richard's responsibility, and he was a professional worrier. If there was anything to worry about, he could worry for both of them. She went to the door and called, 'Coffee!' and he called, 'Right!' in a strange echoing voice from one of the empty rooms upstairs.

He came down carrying his last gleanings in a cardboard carton which he put down in a corner of the kitchen. He seemed quite cheerful now that the dismantling was over. The early colonists had probably thrown a party when they had burned their boats on the new-found beach and there was nothing left but the green hills inland. He said, 'That's the lot,' and came and sat down at the table to drink his coffee.

Kate said, 'Are you going to wear a gown?'

'Good God, I shouldn't think so, not at Glenaidon. Neither a gown nor a kilt. Certainly not both at once, though that would be quite something. Not but what I'm entitled to wear one. A gown, I mean, not a kilt. Which I expect is more than can be said for some of my colleagues.'

She said, 'Richard, it's not all that ropey, is it?'

'Not ropey at all. I've told you. Just not very academic. But who wants to be academic, anyway?'

'What about the boys, then?'

'Well, I haven't seen them yet, of course, but they'll be all right. No lack of discipline, after all. It's not that sort of cranky. Less trouble than the Malembos, I expect. Only of course I didn't have to teach them history. Anyway, it must be far pleasanter teaching history if you don't have to worry too much about exam results. I think I'll enjoy it.' He looked at her, a little cautiously. He said, 'It's you I worry about.'

P. M. HUBBARD

Impatience overcame her suddenly, and she put her cup down in the saucer with a small sharp clink. 'Oh, for God's sake,' she said. 'Look, I agreed to the thing and I've made up my mind to it. I'm not worrying. All right, it may not work. It may not work for you. It may not work for me, though I can't think how. If it doesn't work, we'll have to look at it again. But give it a chance. If you worry about me, it only makes me feel guilty, and that's not fair.'

Her impatience always managed to take him by surprise. Even when he ought to have expected it, it disarmed and mortified him. 'No?' he said. 'No, I suppose not, now you put it like that. All right, I won't worry about you, I promise. But if you can't stand it, just sing out.'

'Sing out be damned. I'll scream so loud you'll hear the purple glens replying. But not unless I've really got something to scream about. Until I do, take it that my heart's in the Hielands, all appearances to the contrary. It may be, yet. I said so just now.'

He let his breath go in a small sigh, and nodded and got up. 'All right. You pack up the coffee things and I'll put the rest of the stuff in the car.' He went out into the hall, and she heard him discussing quietly with himself what he should take first. When he had made up his mind, he opened the front door and dragged a box against it to hold it open. It had never stayed open on its own, not all the time they had been in the house, and now the brass doorstop they had always used had gone with the rest of the stuff. He took the first of the waiting boxes and went down the steps to the car. She gathered up the coffee things and took them to the sink.

With only Richard and herself in the house, she had never been what they called tied to the sink, but she had spent a certain amount of time there, and it was her province. She was a good and careful washer up. So was Richard if the need arose, but she preferred to be left to

6

herself. As with so much else, he accepted this but did not trade on it. Now she was there for the last time. She ought to feel something, relief or regret or even resentment, but she felt nothing at all, or only the usual mild, detached curiosity at her own lack of feeling. She stowed the things in the basket and went across the hall. Richard was just picking up his last load, and she followed him down the steps and put the basket with the rest in the car. The front door, deprived of its stop, swung gently shut behind them. It was as if the house, too, had no particular regrets.

Richard went back up the steps, but she stayed by the car. He opened the door, put his hand inside and released the latch-lock. Then he turned and looked down at her. He looked solemn and slightly baffled, as if the occasion called for some comment, but he could not think what. He made, as he always made, a kindly and distinguished figure, and she wanted to help him out of his difficulty. She could not think of anything to say either, but she smiled at him. He smiled back at her, relieved. Then he pulled the door firmly shut behind him and came down the steps. He did not say anything at all.

Only later, when they had had their hotel dinner and retired to their hotel bedroom, he said, 'I'm sorry about the house.' He was propped up against the pillows in one of the twin beds, watching her as she brushed her hair.

She stopped brushing and looked at him, not directly, but in the glass over the dressing-table. 'Why sorry?' she said.

He was at a loss again now, as he had been when they were still outside the front door, only this time he had committed himself to speech and had to go on with it. 'I don't know. Sorry to leave it, I suppose. It hasn't done us badly.'

She went on brushing her hair. She knew his trick of personalising inanimate things. It was a man's trick, almost entirely. They were detached with people, but treated their possessions as if they were pet dogs. He did not regret leaving the house; he felt guilty because he had abandoned it. But she did not want to argue with him. She said, 'It's done us very well. But we can't live there for fun. It was the job that was wrong. It's the job we're leaving. The house is only incidental.'

He seemed comforted. He settled down slightly on the pillows. 'You're perfectly right,' he said. 'So long as you don't regret it.'

She held her breath for a moment, brushing her hair with a few strokes of unnecessary violence and looking herself firmly in the eye in the glass. Then she said, 'I shan't regret it. Not unless the Glenaidon house is too awful. And you say it's not.'

'It's not awful at all. It's very different, of course, but it's rather nice. I think you'll like it.'

She stopped brushing and put the brush down on the dressing-table. She looked herself over, deliberately and unselfconsciously, in the glass. She thought, 'I really look very nice.' It almost surprised her. She turned away from the dressing-table and took off her dressing-gown. She no longer felt unselfconscious. She threw the dressing-gown across the foot of her bed. 'Let's see, anyhow,' she said. When she went up the alley-way between the beds, he put out an arm to her, and she got into his bed, not hers.

They never talked about their love-making. They never had, and it did not seem to matter. He had taught her all he knew, and they had found out more for themselves, but they never talked about it. Sometimes if he thought he had hurt her, he would say 'Sorry' or 'All right?', and sometimes she would tell him if her leg had gone to sleep or he had his elbow on her hair, but they never talked about the thing itself. It would have seemed like an intrusion on each other's privacy, even if it was the private experience of a shared pleasure. Her body responded to his love-making in what she took to be the normal way, and unless she was tired or unwell, her body was ready for it when it was offered. If it was not ready, he saw this and accepted it. There did not seem to be anything that needed talking about.

He was already drowsy when she got out of bed and left him. That was a bad sign, because when he fell asleep too quickly, he was inclined to wake up an hour or two later and be awake the rest of the night. She stood between the beds, conscious of the colder air on her legs and arms and the inevitable small patch of dampness where she had pulled her nightdress down to save the hotel sheet. The light was out now, but a reflection of the street lighting came faintly between the curtains with the muffled noise of the traffic. They had opened the window a little because the hotel heating was too much for them, and now the room was surprisingly chilly.

Quite deliberately, she roused him before he could fall asleep. She sat herself on the stretched unresponsive sheet and said, 'Lor, the bed's cold.'

He pulled himself obediently up on one elbow and said, 'Sorry. Will you be all right?' There was no question of changing beds, because he always slept on the left.

She got into the bed and pulled the clothes over her. They felt heavy and unfamiliar, but she said, 'Oh yes, I think so. What about you? Are you going to sleep? You've got a long drive tomorrow.'

He let himself flop back on the pillow. 'I almost was,' he said. He wanted her to know she had roused him. He knew that in fact it was no bad thing, but did not, after all these years, suppose that she knew it. She was perpetually surprised at his ignorance of her knowledge of him.

She apologised, duly, in her turn. 'Sorry,' she said. 'You sleep now.'

He grunted and turned over. Kate herself turned a companionable back on him and made herself comfortable. She would in fact be asleep before he was, but now they would both sleep till morning. Then he would be off to Glenaidon.

II

Richard wrote, 'The house is as ready as need be. That is, the furniture is distributed into the most probable rooms, and the small stuff unpacked and provisionally put away. No casualties that I can see, which seems to me good over the distance. It will be up to you to arrange things as you want them. I still like the house, and hope you will. I think I am going to like the H.M. He has enough tongue in his cheek (over the job, I mean) to keep him human. Mrs H. is very bad, and farther south would have lost him the job, I think. Something of a local lassie, raw-skinned and raw-minded, few social graces and not a spark of humour. But I have long given up being surprised at the people people have married. Having said that, let me say that I look forward to having you here. I will meet your train on Friday. Let us hope the sun is out. At this time of the year I admit the country needs it.'

Kate folded the letter and put it back in its envelope. She was slightly uneasy, as she had been before, at the contrast between the acid touch of his pen and the gentleness of his speech and manner. She was sure Mrs Haskell thought him charming. She did not think that made him a hypocrite, and he would fiercely deny hypocrisy. There were two Richards, perhaps, the Richard you talked to and the Richard on paper. Probably more, but those two at least. She wondered whether Richard on paper was the real one, or whether neither was any more real than the other. She wondered whether the amiable, uncommunicative Richard she ate and slept with had words in the back of his mind he never spoke, words for her and what she said and did and what they did together. In any case, it was no good being uneasy about it. It never worried her when they were together, and he did not often have occasion to write to her. And it cut both ways. He wrote that he would be glad to see her. When he got off the train, he would not tell her he was. He would not say a thing like that, only write it. Whether that made it any the more likely to be true she did not know.

She tore the letter up in the evening, before the taxi came to take her to King's Cross. It would not be right to have Richard's letter still in her bag when she met Richard himself, and she would not read it again even if she had it. She was full of apprehensions now, the sort of small vague apprehensions that made up so much of her stock in trade of unpleasant emotion. The trouble with a second-class sleeper was that you had to share it with somebody. It was a long time since she had shared sleeping quarters with another woman, and she did not like the idea. But when it came to the point, she had the sleeper to herself. She made herself attractive but unapproachable to the attendant, ordered tea for the morning and locked herself in. She was still amusing herself with the fittings when the train pulled out. It began to lurch and clatter over the tangled suburban track, and she realised she would be better off in her berth. The water sloshed about in the basin, but it was hot and clean. She washed herself and put on a nightdress, which she had to fish out of her suitcase because she had not expected to be able to get properly to bed. She could not brush her hair properly in the narrow, swinging cabin, but she made a pass at it. Then she looked herself over, as she did every night, in the very effective glass, holding on to one edge of the top berth to steady herself.

She admired herself in the detached, independent way she did now, comfortably aware in one corner of her mind of the small pocket of male admiration down at the end of the corridor. She had expected obtrusive and uncongenial female company, and now she had this locked and vibrating privacy and a man, polite but with his eye cocked, to bring her tea in the morning, which was all she wanted of him. However it was going to finish, the journey had started well. She put out all the lights except the small one over the pillow in the bottom berth. She got into bed and sorted out the heavy railway blankets. Then she put the last light out and lay back, letting the train vibrate northwards under her. She felt powerless but submissive. She did not know at all what Glenaidon was going to do to her, but nothing, anyhow, could do very much. She remembered what Richard had said about the stirring of her Highland blood. All it could manage at the moment was a faint fifty-fifty mixture of amusement and apprehension. The wheels settled down to their steady long-haul rhythm, and the train ran smoothly over them. She could never sleep with this racket going on, but it did not worry her unduly. She slept almost at once.

Once or twice during the night the train stopped. The lack of movement woke her, and she heard echoing voices and saw lights through the blinds over the window. She missed the hiss of escaping steam which had been the voice of a stopped train during her impressionable years, but somewhere away at the head of a long line of cars the diesel throbbed with the same feeling of impatience. Then the train jerked forward and the wheels took up their rhythm again, and she let herself slip back into sleep. She felt lost but perfectly secure. She might be anywhere, but Richard would meet the train in the morning, and then she could deal with things as they came. When she woke for the last time, the train was still moving, and the light outside the windows was daylight. She rolled out from under the blankets and found the air cold. She clutched her nightdress round her and groped in the grey light to turn on the heating which she had turned off at King's Cross. Then she went to the window and pulled the blind up.

A cold weight settled suddenly into the pit of her stomach. The whole world outside was black and utterly desolate. Enormous hills stood up all along the sky, devoid of colour except for the silver threads of falling water. The air between was full of moving clouds of darkness, less palpable than rain, but falling with the downward drag of moisture on to the total emptiness of the moor. There was nothing anywhere for the eye to rest on, not a house, not a tree, not a road, not even a path through the wilderness. The train ran steadily on, aiming to get somewhere at the end of it all, and she was seized with a panic that it might stop before it got there. She shivered violently, jerked the blind down and scrambled back under the blankets.

There was no more sleep to be had. All she could do was to keep warm in her berth until the heater had taken the chill out of the air. According to her watch it was another hour and a half before they were due at Glenaidon. Some time before then she would presumably get her tea. The man had her ticket and knew where she was getting out. Another hour and a half, and the train was going a fair pace. The size of the desolation appalled her. It was not her Highland blood that was stirring, it was the old horrors she had picked up from her father and never quite forgotten. Nearly all his stories were horrible, even the ones he had told her. Like many Highlanders, he had taken an obscure, jocular pride in the barbarous history of his country. There was always treachery and violence in the stories, and the blood was given a special mention. Burns that ran red with blood and stains that would not come clean. They had been no more than fairy stories to her then, but something of the horror had stuck, and in a country like this anything was possible. She knew it was nonsense, but the depression was real and would not go. She snuggled down under the

14

blankets, concentrating for assurance on the small dark Londoner who presently would bring tea.

Warmth was the thing. She could cope with anything so long as she did not get cold. She fell into a half doze, knowing that the compartment was getting warmer and the light outside was growing. The train stopped twice, very briefly, at what must have been stations, but she did not rouse herself to look out. Then someone knocked on the door, a single violent thump, and a voice outside said something she did not understand. She reached out an arm and slipped the bolt, and as she got back under the blankets the roof light was clicked on and a man came in carrying a tray. He was not her small neat man of the night before, but a bigger man with sandy hair and a red skin. He pulled out the flap table and put the tray on it. He said something as he put the tray down. She caught the name Glenaidon despite the unfamiliar pronunciation, but the rest she could not follow. The old panic of being addressed in a foreign language gripped her. She said, 'I'm sorry?', peering up at him, and he looked down at her with a sort of exasperated impatience, as if she was being stupid.

He said, 'You'll be getting out at Glenaidon?'

'Yes,' she said, 'yes, that's right.'

He nodded, as if he had made some progress. He said, 'We'll be there in half an hour, maybe.'

'Oh,' she said. 'Yes. Thank you very much.'

He was still looking at her as if he was not quite sure she had understood. There was no deference in the look, only a touch of what seemed sardonic amusement. Then he nodded again and went out, slamming the door shut behind him. Richard's phrase came into her head, raw-skinned and raw-minded. She slipped back the bolt of the door. She felt ruffled and once more depressed, but at least the compartment was getting warm and she had her tea.

The tea was bitter and black, but it was hot, and when

she threw off the blankets for the last time, she had all the warmth she wanted. She pulled off her nightdress in the cosy, brilliantly lit cabin, and went over and looked at herself in the glass. Nude in a sleeper. Russell Flint stuff, barely out of the pin-up class, dark hair, elegant smallish breasts, cream-coloured skin. She posed suggestively and caught herself smiling wryly at the result. But she could not get out like this, least of all at Glenaidon. She started to dress. Already she felt more cheerful. She had never been in a really hot country, and wondered if there was any point at which her spirits would stop rising with the temperature. She was almost ready when it occurred to her to switch the light off. The daylight outside the blinds was golden yellow. She pulled the blind up and said, 'Oh.' The whole landscape was full of sunlight.

Even through the railway glass the air looked marvellously transparent. Not clear, like lowland air after rain, because here the air itself seemed visible. It was more like fantastically translucent water. There were mountains now, surely those must rank as mountains, gold and brown and buff, and fading back through every shade of grey to an almost perfect blue, and all awash with this extraordinary visible but translucent vapour. She wrestled with the stiff catch and then slid the glass itself down. It moved six inches and then stuck, but six inches was enough. She put her face to the gap, so that the slanting sunlight just caught her nose, and the smell of the moor flooded into the compartment. It was a brown smell, unlike any of the green and yellow smells she associated with open country. It had the breath of perennial decay in it, but a decay without offence. She was used to deciduous woodlands, but here the whole landscape was deciduous, so that even in this autumn sunlight there was next to no green anywhere. No wonder if under a grey sky it looked almost black.

She realised that the train was slowing down and, leaning

out a little, saw a couple of houses ahead. This was it. She tried to get the glass up, failed and turned back in a hurry to put the finishing touches to herself and get her things together. As she slid the door back, she saw the name Glenaidon, in white letters on blue, go slowly past the corridor window. Then the train stopped.

She bundled her suitcases along the corridor, got the door open and stepped out on to a disconcertingly empty platform. It was a tiny station, but the train had shrunk during the night to a mere three coaches, and the platform was long enough. Away at the head of the train a man wearing a railway jacket and a deerstalker cap was talking to the driver. Half-way along, opposite the first-class coach, a gaunt figure in drab tweeds stood completely motionless, relaxed but expectant, like a cat at a mousehole. There was no sign of Richard. Then the door at the near end of the first-class coach swung open with dramatic violence, and an expensive man got out.

The expensiveness was the first thing she noticed. It started with the suitcase which he swung out ahead of him and spread up through a gold wristwatch to include faultlessly casual tweeds and a mild contented blue eye. Nice expensive, she thought. His money had not spoilt him yet, but he took it very much for granted. He was fairish, somewhere in his forties and damnably well preserved. The figure along the platform came smoothly to life, and the man said, 'Ah, morning, Alec.' Then he turned and looked at Kate.

It was an extremely practised look, friendly, politely deferential, missing nothing. She was immediately conscious that her final preparations had been rushed. She had been expecting Richard. She smiled at him. There was nothing else to do with a look like that. He smiled back, opening his eyes slightly, as if he liked what he saw and wanted to have a better look at it. 'Good morning,' he said.

'Are you being met?' The voice went with the rest of him. There did not seem to be anything Highland in it.

She said, 'Oh yes. My husband will be along. I expect he's been held up.' She was very conscious of being alone in the middle of a vast sunlit wilderness, but she had no intention of doing a waif-and-stray act for his benefit.

He nodded. 'Right,' he said. 'If you're sure. But my car's here. I don't know where —'

'I'm going to the school,' she said.

His head went up, as if he had the answer that had been eluding him. 'Oh, the school, of course. I was wondering – I haven't seen you before.'

She said, 'I haven't been here before.' She heard, in the enormous silence, Richard's feet hurrying over the footbridge from the other side of the line. There was no mistaking his walk, even on a railway footbridge. She took her eyes off the contented blue eyes and caught, as she turned, the eye of the man called Alec. His eyes were yellow-brown in a bony, weather-beaten face, and they were looking at her with a sort of expectant amusement. He would be the expensive man's retainer, a keeper or something of the sort, only up here she thought they called it a stalker, and she thought to hell with his expectation and his amusement. His laird was a charmer, all right, but his sporting rights were not unlimited.

Richard said, 'Hullo, Kate. Awfully sorry. The damned car wouldn't start. It took a bit of a beating on the way up, and I haven't had time to get it seen to. Good journey?' His eyes went beyond her to the expensive man. She hoped Alec had taken the smile off his face.

The man said, 'Good morning. We haven't met. My name's Macalister. I was just asking your wife if she had transport.'

Richard said, 'Good morning. Wychett. Very kind of you. But I've got the car here at last.' He walked past her

18

and solemnly shook hands with Mr Macalister. He had not touched her yet. She watched them with the fascination she never failed to feel at this first cautious meeting of two civilised Englishmen. Only here one of them was presumably a Scot. Like the encounter of two dog-apes. Jacques had seen the fascination of it, too, in another, more southerly, wilderness.

Mr Macalister said, 'Good. I hope we shall see something of you now you're here. We need new faces in the glen.' He spoke entirely to Richard. He did not look at Kate at all. Alec was looking at Richard, too. His face was completely impassive, with the lines of melancholy or alcohol drawn deeply down the sides of his mouth. He reminded her of a dog, fierce but disciplined, watching the man his master is talking to. She did not like him.

Richard said, 'That would be nice. You'll know where to find me.' He said me, not us, as if there was an understanding between them to ignore Kate's existence. Then he turned back to her, and as he turned both master and man looked at her again. Neither face changed. Alec included her in his inscrutable observation and Mr Macalister in his friendliness. This time she did not smile back at him.

Richard had her suitcases now. She said, 'Is it far?'

'Twenty minutes or so. It's a nice run. I'm glad the sun's come out for you.'

Another man came out of the station building. He had a cap with gold braid about it, and a polite serious face. He said, 'May I have your ticket, please?'

She gave it to him, and followed Richard along the platform towards the bridge. She wondered why she had not smiled at Mr Macalister, and why she was glad she had not.

III

The wind blew steadily in her face as she went up the hill. It had struck cold when she first came out, but by now she would be much too hot without it. She scrambled up a steeper slope, using her hands to get a purchase on the heather when her feet threatened to go from under her, so that at times she was almost crawling. It would not be dignified, especially from behind, but there was no one behind her, not for half a mile or so in distance and several hundred feet in height. In itself it was mildly exhilarating. It was years since she had consciously exerted her physical strength like this. There was nothing in the life of the town to make you do it, and she was no games player. Now she was panting and slightly sweaty, and the muscles in the back of her legs twanged like piano wires. It made her feel very young, and it was all right so long as no one could see her. She flopped down on a hummock of grey rock and turned to look back at the school.

It had not been built as a school, obviously. It had been built as some Edwardian's idea of a Highland castle, all pepper-pot turrets and battlements not quite hiding the dormer windows of the servants' rooms up under the slates. All the same, it had come off much better than it deserved, simply because of its position. The setting was breathtaking, and a soberer building might have wasted it. The river ran shallow and sparkling in front of the house, with only a stretch of grass between them. The grass was regimented now, laid out in blocks and patterns for the school games, but from up here you could not see the details, only the wide green stretch between the house and the river.

Behind the house, southwards, the side of the glen went up steeply in pinewoods, with the houses of the staff tucked in among them. They had cut out little shelves for them in the hill-face, with an interconnecting system of stepped foot-paths and roads which were a little alarming but just about motorable. It was all very expensive and in very good taste, except for the main house itself, which had also, in its day, been expensive, but was in the taste of another generation. She tried to identify her house, but could not be certain. Eastwards the glen opened out, and she could just see the steely glitter of the loch. Westwards it climbed and narrowed, and there was nothing to see but hills. It was all grey and brown under a dappled grey sky. She felt much more remote from the school than the mere distance justified. It was the difference in height and the huge extent of the desolation and silence round her. At any rate, she was glad of it. She had already seen enough of the school to know that she would need this facility in getting away from it. What she was aiming at was to get over the top of the hill and out of sight of the school altogether. She could see already that this was going to be harder than it had looked from below.

She had got her breath back now and was starting to feel the edge of the wind again. She got up and turned back to her climb. There was nothing to stop her. It was just a matter of keeping going. There was a bunch of grey crags on the skyline which she thought must be the top. She could see her way clear to it, but she knew by now that it would be farther than it looked.

She stopped once more just under the final slope. When she looked back at the school, the place had come alive, with minute figures scurrying everywhere. It must be the mid-morning break, but the general effect was so like a disturbed ants' nest that it was difficult to consider it in human terms. The smaller figures moved especially fast,

21

because it was one of the school things that the boys ran from place to place outside the buildings. Between these racing dots of colour larger and darker figures, the queens or drones of the nest, moved more slowly as the staff headed for their houses or the common-room. One of them might be Richard, but she could not pick him out any more than she could pick their house out of the clustered boxes on the hill-face. She wondered suddenly whether she, alone on her hill, might not be visible, even conspicuous, to some of those horribly long-sighted eyes milling about all that way below. She did not want them to see her. It would be no good her losing sight of the school, if the school, right up to the last, had not lost sight of her. It would be all right if she kept still. She sank down instinctively behind the rock she had been going to sit on and stayed there, crouching, with just the top of her head clear of the grey stone, peering over it and waiting for the distant excitement to subside.

She knew, in the more civilised part of her mind, that this was an odd thing to do. She did not want to have to explain, to Richard or anyone else, even why she had come all this way up the north face of the glen. She certainly did not want to explain what she was doing crouching behind a rock, trying not to be seen. She did not try to explain this, even to herself. It was just the effect the place had on her and she rather enjoyed it. Nothing to do with her Highland blood – that she insisted on. It was more a matter of acting wild in a wilderness, as children scout in a wood or disappear under the bushes of an unkempt garden. She crouched there, content and rather feline, watching the school go about its business down there by the river. It was only when it was all quiet again that she got up and resumed her climb.

She worked her way up a ribbon of turf in a cleft of the rock, and when her head came level with the top, there was no more hill above her, and the wind was blowing horizontally through her hair. She pulled herself up on to the rock and stopped, awe-struck. A vast reach of broken and empty country stretched away to the northern mountains, and in the foreground, hardly fifty yards from her, a herd of deer was grazing. Or had been grazing. Now they all flung their heads up and looked at her. There must have been twenty or thirty of them, with a big stag to one side of the group. For an endless moment of time they stood there, eyes staring, nostrils dilated, great ears turned to pick up whatever sound was associated with this sudden movement. Then the rifle fired.

It was so loud and startling that it destroyed all her concentration. She jerked her head to the right, where the shot had come from. When she turned back, the deer had gone, all but the stag. He still stood there, with his head tilted back, balancing the enormous weight of his antlers. He looked mildly startled. Then he trotted straight towards her. There was no hurry in it. He did not seem to be very certain what he was at. He trotted quietly for a dozen paces, and then his head dropped and he pitched straight down into the heather. He did not move at all where he lay. She could just see a grey-brown curve of flank and one antler standing up stiffly from the fallen head. It was all sudden and appalling and quite conclusive. The stag was dead, not forty yards from her, and she was no longer alone.

Mr Macalister and the man Alec were coming towards her over the heather. After a little they separated. Alec made for the stag and Mr Macalister made for her. He still had the rifle in his hands. She stood there, utterly unnerved, and watched him come. He slung his rifle over one shoulder and raised his tweed cap politely. He said, 'You startled me. I didn't see you until after I had fired. I saw their heads go up, but I didn't know what had done it. What are you doing, wandering about up here by yourself?'

'You startled me,' said Kate. 'Is there any reason why I

shouldn't come up here?'

He was close to her now. He stood looking her over with his steady, confident eyes. She had never seen anyone look less startled in her life. 'Well,' he said, 'you're on my land, of course. But there's no law of trespass in Scotland. The thing is, it can be a nuisance. It could even be dangerous. At this time of the year, I mean, when the stalking's still on. If you had come over the top a couple of seconds earlier, I'd have lost that beast, and I've been out after him most days for the past week. And of course if you'd managed to get into the line of fire, you might have got hit.'

She said, 'I'm afraid I wish you had lost him. I saw him very close. I couldn't bear to see him go down like that.'

He shook his head. 'He didn't know what hit him. Not a bad way to die. Better than disease and old age. He was in his prime. Come and look at him. He's got a fine head.'

She did not move. 'As a matter of fact,' she said, 'I don't believe he did. Know what hit him, I mean. He was very dignified about it.'

'They are, the big stags. They're splendid beasts.' He turned and started back towards Alec and the fallen deer.

'And yet you shoot them,' she said. She still had not moved. He stopped and turned round to face her again.

'Oh yes,' he said. 'They've got to be shot. The thing is to do it properly. There's plenty of people who aren't so particular.'

He was perfectly matter-of-fact about it. She still felt indignant, but was beginning to feel a little foolish. He turned and walked off again, and this time she went after him. He heard her coming and waited for her. They came up to the stag together, with Alec crouched beside it, watching them as they came. He had a long knife in his hand. He said, 'Will I do the gralloch, Mr James?'

'Yes,' said Mr Macalister, 'but hold on a minute. I want to show Mrs Wychett the beast.'

The man turned his tawny eyes and looked at Kate. She was reminded again of an animal, docile but potentially fierce. She did not expect to have any communication with him except through his master. His eyes went backwards and forwards between the two of them, puckered and speculative. He said, 'Ay,' and turned and drove the knife into the turf beside him. Then he caught hold of the upturned antler and swung the great head over until it was stretched out upright, with the horns standing up above it. The eyes were velvet brown and wide open, staring at nothing. There was no blood, but the rank, sweet smell of the beast was everywhere. 'Yon's a fine head,' the man said. 'There's eleven points. I doubt he's gone back a bit. If we'd had him last year, he'd have been a royal, maybe.'

Mr Macalister nodded. 'Maybe,' he said. He looked at Kate. 'The antlers come bigger every year,' he said, 'up to a certain age. Then they can get smaller again, so long as the beast survives. I said he was in his prime. He may have been just past it, in fact.'

She did not say anything. She was still looking down at the outstretched head and the wide eyes. She felt full of pity, but as death went it was all very tidy and free of offence. When she looked up, she found Mr Macalister watching her. He was smiling very slightly, but she was conscious of an odd sympathy in him, even though it was he who had done the shooting. 'Sorry,' he said. 'You could have done without the nature notes. Come on. I'll see you on your way.' He took her by the arm and turned her to face the way they had come. 'You carry on, Alec,' he said. 'I'll be back to give you a hand with him.' They started to walk towards the rocks at the edge of the face. After a few paces he took his hand off her arm, and they walked side by side in silence. The indignation had gone out of her, but she felt curiously shaken. It was clearly time she said something, but she could not think of anything to say.

25

What she did say surprised her as much as it did him. She said, 'What an odd man that is.'

'Alec?' he said. He thought for a moment. 'Yes, I suppose he is. I'm used to him, of course. But he'll be an unfamiliar type to you, obviously. He's a hard drinker, for one thing. They mostly are. They don't start on beer, as they do down south. They start straight away on the hard stuff, and by his age they're practically living on it. It doesn't seem to do them any harm. He's a marvel on the hill, whatever state he's in. He was my father's stalker, and of course I've always had him.' He turned and looked at her for a moment. 'You don't like him?' he said.

They had come out on to the top of the rocks. The school lay at their feet, but showed no signs of life. The cloud had thickened and the whole glen was full of a soft translucent murk. They stopped. Kate said, 'No, I don't think I do.'

'Ah,' he said. 'You'll get used to us.' There was a touch of Highland in it. He did not quite say 'Och', but the sound was one no Englishman would have made. Whether it was deliberate she did not know. His normal speech was impeccable southern English. He said, 'It's a strange part of the world for the English person, especially seeing it for the first time. We're all a bit mad by southern standards. But you'll get used to us.'

Kate was not having this. She had been this way before, long ago. In another minute, she thought, he'll be telling me how an ancestor of his killed three female Mackintoshes with a single sword-cut and hung their breasts on an oak tree. And the blood—She said, 'I'm not English, in fact. Or only on my mother's side.'

He nodded. He was smiling again as he looked at her. They stood there on top of the rocks, and it occurred to her that they must be enormously visible from below, more than life-size figures stuck up on the towering skyline. 'You're not?' he said.

26

'My father was a Macinnes. I've had the full treatment.' She had an uneasy feeling that she might be sounding a little shrill, but if she was, he did not seem to notice it.

'A Macinnes?' he said. 'Your country's away south and west of here, then. Your husband called you Kate. You'll have been christened Catherine, of course. Kate's very English.'

Damn the man, she thought. But there was no way out. 'Catriona,' she said.

'Catriona. Catriona Macinnes.' He pronounced the name as her father had pronounced it. Admittedly, it sounded less arty-crafty like that than it did in English, but she had much rather he did not pronounce it at all. 'I knew there was something,' he said.

She wanted to say, 'There's not,' but even in her present mood of despairing exasperation she knew that this was too childish to let pass. She said, 'I much prefer Kate,' but he took no notice of this at all.

'It's the cheekbones,' he said, 'and the nose, of course. That and the colouring.'

She could not give him the lie on this. She remembered her dark aquiline father too well for that. Her mother had been as blonde and blue-eyed as Mr Macalister himself was. She found this confusing and unfair, but to point out the discrepancy would involve her in the sort of personalities she was most anxious to avoid. She abandoned the point and said, 'I must be getting back. And you must go and help Alec with the stag.' She thought for a moment, and curiosity, a simple wish to know, overcame her. 'Help him how?' she said.

He laughed at this. It was the first time she had heard him laugh. It was not much more than a chuckle, but full of enormous good humour. 'Drag it,' he said. 'That beast will weigh a good twenty stone, and the Land-Rover's half a mile away. You can't carry them. You put a rope on and drag them. Or you can use a pony with a proper saddle, but that means an extra man. They make a special trolley, but they're more trouble than they're worth. Or of course nowadays you can get powered vehicles that are supposed to go over anything, but I don't fancy them. It's always been dragging on the hill, that or ponies. And ponies cost more to keep than they did. So do pony men. Anyway, dragging's part of the game. Makes you work for your beast. Also, of course, it makes you a lot more careful about where you shoot them.'

The educated townswoman in her threw up some comment about sado-masochism, but she did not really believe that Mr Macalister was either a sadist or a masochist. He was a primitive, a civilised primitive. She labelled him and left him. She said again, 'I must be going. Goodbye, Mr Macalister.'

He doffed his cap as politely as he had when they met. He said, 'Goodbye now, Mistress Wychett.' This was pure calculated Highland, but the mockery was a very mild one. At least he had not called her Catriona. She nodded and started to scramble down the hill-face. For a moment or two she felt his eyes on her back, but by the time she let herself turn round he was gone.

IV

The pudding was a trifle with little macaroon biscuits scattered over the top. All the four men ate it differently. Mr Haskell ate his with a sort of studious detachment, that offered no comment and invited none. Of the two young men, the fair one did not seem to notice what he was eating at all. His name was something that sounded like Baysford. He was rather pink and plump, and he concentrated his entire attention on Kate. When on occasion she caught his eye, he gave her an enormous smile. It was a commonplace to compare young men with large dogs, but this went too far altogether. Every Labrador she met for the rest of her life would remind her of Mr Baysford. The dark one, Mr Godwin, was very different. He detached individual macaroons deliberately from their cream setting and chased them round the plate with his fork with an air of intense and secret amusement. His big green eyes offered to share this amusement with her, but on strictly equal terms. He was not subject to her at all. Richard ate his trifle with an elegant thoroughness, though when she caught his eye, there was a gleam in it. She wondered how long it was since he had eaten trifle with little macaroons on top. In fact he was enjoying it, but he would be telling himself that he was carrying off Mrs Haskell's food with an air, and he would be mildly amusing about it when they got home.

The men wore ordinary dark suits and Kate her short black. Mrs Haskell's dress was satin of an electric blue that met her ruddy skin with startling violence at the neckline. It rustled when she moved, and its highlights threw up the contours of her tremendous figure. This was something

Kate had not expected at all. Richard's account had suggested rather an angular woman. In fact it was only her mind that was angular, though the harshness of her mind had stamped itself on a face which otherwise might have gone with the body. The whole effect was that of a Salvation Army lass with the body of a Rubens Venus. But at least Kate knew why Mr Haskell had married her. These slight, intense men had to have their pound of flesh, whether it was a blowsy trollop like Emma Hamilton or a Salvation lassie like Janet Haskell. Their minds must surely be too intelligent and too fastidious not to know, later, what they had done, but even then the physical need seemed paramount. She liked Mr Haskell and felt very sorry for him. Nevertheless, she was not at all sure that he was consciously in need of pity.

He said, 'You've met the laird, I take it?'

'Macalister?' said Richard. 'Yes, we met him at the station. He came up on Kate's train. Are we on his domains here?'

'Not this side of the river. This was Paterson land originally, but a man called Garston bought the place and built the house. He was in trade of some sort.'

'Biscuits,' said Mrs Haskell.

'Biscuits, that's right. Of course, a place in the Highlands was just the thing then. Hence the baronial features.'

'I rather like it,' said Kate. 'In the setting, I mean. It looks fine from the other side of the glen.'

Mr Haskell turned and looked at her. He smiled slightly. It was a schoolmaster's trick, perhaps, looking at a person with a sort of pleasant detachment while you considered what it was you wanted to say to them. It assumed a captive audience, but she found it rather endearing. She smiled back at him and waited. He did not really take very long to make up his mind. It was just that the intervals were there. First the look, then the smile, then the words. He said,

'You've been exploring?'

'Not very far,' she said. 'Just over the bridge and a bit up the other side.'

Mrs Haskell said, 'Now there you were on Macalister's land. All that side of the water from near the head of the glen to half-way down the loch. He'll have twenty thousand acres, about. And the lodge at Bridge of Aidon. He's quite the fine gentleman, is Macalister.'

Kate looked at her helplessly. She thought, it's up to her husband to get us out of this. He must be used to it. She would not catch Richard's eye, but she knew he was looking at her. Instead she caught Mr Godwin's. It was full of impish delight, and she looked away again.

Mr Haskell continued to smile. He spoke very gently and evenly. He said, 'Janet doesn't approve of the laird. He sold his birthright for a mess of pottage. A pretty rich mess, by all accounts. I can't say I hold it quite so strongly against him. He probably needed the money. They're fine and feudal, these Highland estates, but they don't bring in much. There's no tenantry, you see.'

Richard said, 'Where was this, then? If he's still got twenty thousand acres and half the glen, he can't have sold all that much, surely?'

'No, well, that's it, really. They had this bit of land on the far side of the loch, a few hundred acres. I don't know how they got it originally. Some marriage, probably. But right across the water, you see, well away from the rest of their land. It doesn't worry Macalister what goes on there. But it upset the rest of the glen no end.'

'But what does go on there?' said Kate. 'Who did he sell it to? A nudist colony, or something?'

Mr Baysford looked shocked. Mr Godwin said, 'They wouldn't have minded that. They're all great stalkers.' Kate caught his eye again, and this time they both smiled.

Mr Haskell said, 'No, it was Cotton's, the holiday-camp

people. In season it's all chalets and dance halls and bingo parlours and water skiing on the loch. It's a marvellous site for them, of course. But – well, you can imagine.'

'Lord,' said Kate, 'I can indeed. I shouldn't have thought he'd have been allowed to.'

Mrs Haskell said, 'Oh, the Tourist Board was all for it. It was the old laird who wouldn't sell. Then he died, and Master James had his lawyers on to it before the old man was well buried.'

'In fact,' said Mr Haskell, 'I'm not sure it does much good – I mean, not in proportion to the disturbance it creates. It gives some employment, of course. Half our domestic staff desert us in the season and then expect to be able to come back in the winter. But I don't know that it brings much money in otherwise. They have their own wholesale suppliers, obviously. And the campers don't spend anything outside. They pay their inclusive charges and have their fun inside the wire, when they aren't wandering about on the hill. Or out on the water. And of course speedboats on the loch don't improve the fishing, and community revels on the hillside don't improve the shooting or the stalking. And, as I said, that's all you get from the land. Even in terms of money, I mean. It's not only a matter of the gentlemen losing their sport. Many of them aim to make a bit by letting the sporting rights in a gentlemanly sort of way, and Macalister's gain is their loss. It's not only the honour of the glen that's touched, it's its pocket. And they're both pretty sensitive in these parts.'

Kate said, 'In the old days Mr Macalister would have found a dirk in his back one dark night.'

Mrs Haskell looked at her with sudden approval, as if she had found an unexpected ally. 'He would that,' she said. 'As it is, he's doing well enough.' She shook her fierce head at the decadence of the age.

'I thought he looked very prosperous,' said Kate. 'That

32

was the first thing that struck me about him. Quite the fine gentlemen, as you said.'

'Yes,' said Mr Haskell. 'I doubt if anyone really knows the details of the deal. The whisper in the glen —'

Mrs Haskell's head snapped up and she made a very small impatient sound. Mr Haskell looked at her, smiling, and then included the others in his smile. The same trick, thought Kate. Playing to a captive audience. Richard said, 'The whisper in the glen. I like that. The local grapevine, I suppose.'

Mr Haskell said, 'Bush telegraph is perhaps nearer. They say that if you set out early in the morning and drive to the other end of the glen, the first person you meet will know what you had for breakfast.'

Mr Godwin said, 'In point of fact, the first three people you meet will be ready to say what you had for breakfast, but they'll all say something different. The one thing you can be sure of is that none of it will be to your advantage.'

Kate said, 'They'd know if you hadn't had any breakfast?'

'Yes,' said Mr Godwin, 'I think they very likely might.' He turned and looked with a sort of elaborate deference at Mr Haskell. 'I'm sorry, sir,' he said. 'I'm afraid I interrupted.'

'Well,' said Mr Haskell, 'the whisper in the glen is that Macalister not only got capital out of the deal with Cotton's. He kept some sort of interest in the place. At any rate, he's a lot more comfortable than he was.'

Richard said, 'The more I hear of your laird, the more interesting he becomes. I must see more of him.' He spoke to the headmaster, and his tone was gently bantering. He's trying to take the heat out of the conversation, thought Kate. One man helping another in a social predicament. They all do it. Especially if a woman's the trouble.

But Mrs Haskell put her head up and looked across the

table at Kate. She looked her over appraisingly, but did not catch her eye. Then she turned and looked at Richard. 'You will,' she said, 'I don't doubt.'

The silence was only momentary, but it made itself felt as a silence. Then Mr Haskell pushed his chair back. 'Well,' he said, 'what about coffee?'

When they had made their adieus and got outside, the cloud had gone and the sky was full of stars. The lights in the school blocks were mostly out, but the windows of the staff houses glowed among the pine branches like the lights on a Christmas tree. Between, and under their feet, it was very dark. The towering hill-face across the river was visible only as an absence of stars. They got clear of the house and stood for a moment, letting their eyes get used to it. If Kate had stumbled, Richard would have put a hand firmly under her elbow, but she did not. She was better in the dark than he was. She thought he was going to be funny, but when he finally spoke, his voice was perfectly serious. He said, 'That's a dangerous woman, Kate. You'll have to watch her.'

She was angry on the instant. She was alarmed to find how often, now, anger was her first reaction to something Richard said, but it was a passing anger and she did not let it show. She waited for a moment. She thought he was looking at her, but she knew that even if he was, he could not see her face. Then she said, 'Oh, I don't think dangerous, really. Awkward as hell, I agree, and not a gleam of humour. But he's good with her. I like him a lot.' She spoke pleasantly, still considering, in the back of her mind, the reasons for her anger and not liking what she found.

She did not think he would pursue the matter, and he did not. They started to walk up the path, and he said, 'Yes, he's a nice chap. Knows his job, too. I imagine he married her after he got here. But he won't want to stay here for ever, and she'd be a bit of a handicap farther south.'

She said, 'That's for him to worry about. I think he can handle her.' They went on for a moment in silence. Then she said, 'Mr Godwin, now. I think he could be dangerous. Amusing, all right, but dangerous.'

'Yes,' said Richard, 'I shouldn't wonder. That sort very often are.'

'That sort? Oh, I see. Yes, you're very likely right. I couldn't quite place it. None of the doglike devotion of Mr Baysford, certainly. More as one woman to another. What does he teach?'

'Junior French, I think. But P.T.'s his real thing. They take it very seriously here. The ordinary games are pretty casual.'

'I see, yes. It fits, I think. The body beautiful and all that. After all, girls get crushes on the games mistress. Or used to. I suppose in these more enlightened days they just go to bed with the games master.'

'I suppose so,' he said. Farther up the hill she did in fact miss her footing, and they came to the house amicably arm in arm.

It was a nice house, even though it was a bungalow, which she did not usually care for. It glowed ready to receive them, and when they got inside, it was warm, warmer than the London house had ever been. She took her coat off and thought how pleasant it was not to miss it. She said, 'What about a nightcap? Just to settle the meal.'

'I don't know. It wasn't as bad a meal as all that.'

'But not a meal to ask a man to?'

He smiled. 'Not really, no. But the wine was all right. I imagine that's his doing.'

'Anyway,' she said, 'a whisky? I could do with one.'

He looked at her a little doubtfully. 'Could you?' he said. 'All right, I'll join you.'

She wondered, as he did, why she wanted a drink. She did not think it was the meal that needed settling, but she would have been upset if he had not had one with her. That was no doubt why he had. There was an odd, uneasy awareness of each other which they were not used to. She took it for granted that when they were ready for bed, they would make love, and they did. Afterwards, when she had roused herself to go back to her own bed, he said suddenly, 'Are you going to like it here?'

There was no anger in her reaction now, only a curious carefulness, as if she had to get the answer right. She said, 'Yes, I think so. I love the place. So big and quiet.'

'The school's anything but quiet.'

'Yes, I expect so. But that's your department, isn't it?'

'That's perfectly true. For what it's worth, I'm enjoying it.'

'I know. That's good.'

He said nothing for a bit, and she thought perhaps he had gone to sleep. Even with the curtains drawn back from the windows the room was marvellously dark. Then he said, 'Well, so long as the place is all right. I told you. Your Highland blood.'

It was a small, deliberate joke, something they could both take refuge in, and she accepted it gratefully. She said, 'Perhaps that's it,' in a small, sleepy voice, and turned over on her side, as she always did, facing away from him. After a bit she knew he was asleep, but she could not sleep herself for quite a long time.

It was the dream that woke her. She dreamed that she was out on the hill. There was a thick mist everywhere, and she did not know which way to go. This was important, because she knew there were people shooting on the moor. She could not hear any shots, but she was afraid she would be shot if she could not find her way home. Then the stag came trotting towards her through the mist. It trotted straight past her, and she saw its brown eyes wide open, but it could not see anything because it had been shot. She thought that at any moment it was going to fall into the heather, and she was terrified. She shouted for Richard, and he came up to her suddenly out of the mist, and she clung to him with immeasurable comfort. They started to make love, there in the heather, but when he was inside her, she looked up at him and saw that it was not Richard but James Macalister. A pang of pure, enormous pleasure, such as she had never known, bit into her, but already she knew that it could not be right, and that it was only a dream. She struggled to hold on to the dream, but there was light on the other side of her eyelids now, and a moment later she was awake and staring at the windows. The sky was full of daylight.

She lay flat on her back, utterly limp and devastated. She wanted to turn on her side and make herself comfortable, but she was afraid that if she moved, she might wake Richard in the next bed, and she could not cope with him until she had got the dream out of her system.

After a bit she turned over, very cautiously, and lay thinking. She was wide awake now, but her heart was still hammering. She tried to come to terms with the fact that her body seemed to have decided, quite independently of her, to have an affair with James Macalister. It had never done that with anybody before. It had not even decided to marry Richard. She had decided that, independently of her body, and it had worked out all right. She did not trust her body's judgement at all. Richard slept on, and it was some time before she could bring herself to wake him. When she did, it was later than it should have been, and there was a rush to get him off to the school.

As he was going off, she said, 'I'm going into Aberwhinnie. I've got shopping to do. I'll be back for lunch.'

'All right,' he said, 'but don't worry if you can't make it. I can always get lunch at the school.' He waved a hand a bit distractedly and went off down the path, hurrying, with his books and papers under his arm. She watched him for quite a long time before she shut the door. She felt as hollow and secret as if she was hurrying off to an assignation, but she was going to Aberwhinnie, which was twenty miles away, and a blameless town of four or five streets full of mediocre shops. She was guilty of nothing more than the aching pleasure of a dream. The situation was ridiculous, but she did not find it funny.

V

At Bridge of Aidon the road divided and went both sides of the loch. She took the right fork along the south shore. The gates of the Lodge were on the north road. She had driven that way once, but the house was back among the trees, and you could not see it from the road. The south road was new to her, and was more difficult driving. It went in a twisting switchback along the side of the loch. She dared not take her eyes off it for long, but she was aware all the time of dark trees piled up on her right and the huge stretch of grey water never very far from the tarmac on her left. There were a few houses and cottages, but she saw no one, and nothing stirred but the sheep. She drove five miles through the silence before she came to the holiday camp, but when she did, she pulled the car in to the side of the road and stopped. She had been determined, almost savagely, to get the full beauty of it, but even at first glance it was start-ling. Here, of all places, it was an outrage.

The slope of the hill-face was gentler here, and she reckoned there would once have been some open space, probably with rough grass and birch shaws on it, between the edge of the pine forest and the road. Whatever there had been, it had been bulldozed flat and covered with con-crete and tarmac. Most of it was car-park, empty now behind the wire fence and entrance gates that fronted the road. Behind the car-park there was a group of communal buildings, not very high, but covering an enormous floor-space. They looked like aircraft hangars, and had the same air of impermanence and improvisation. They had been painted light blue, but already the Highland weather was getting at the paint. Behind them again, where the natural slope of the hill took over from the artificial level, the chalets were packed in dense irregular rows among what was left of the trees. Whatever they were made of, they had the colour and texture of damp linen. All round, outside the tall wire, the trees stood dark and motionless, and above them the hillside ran up to the high, bare skyline of the moor. Inside there was no sign of life except two cars huddled together in a far corner of the empty asphalt. There must be someone living there, but wherever they were, they were not on show. The effect of dereliction was complete.

Kate walked slowly across the road. She put her hands on the wire and stood there, staring through it, speechless and appalled. In summer, no doubt, this damp desolation would be alive with piped music and synthetic jollity, but that would be even worse. For some reason, the person who came into her head was not James Macalister, who had allowed this outrage to happen, but the old laird, who had not been well buried before the thing was done. She did not know where he was buried or what had carried him off so inopportunely, but she felt that the honour of the glen lay buried with him. As for James, she would willingly have put the dirk in his back that Mrs Haskell had so much liked the sound of; but all she seemed able to do was cry out with pleasure in the night because she dreamed he was making love to her. She got back into the car, angrier and more confused than ever, and made an unaccustomed mess of the gears in her eagerness to get away.

Just beyond the camp there was an old stone house, not much more than a cottage, standing a little back from the road. It was a decent, solid little house. Not so long ago it would have been somebody's home, but now disaster had overtaken it along with the rest of the place. The doors and window frames had been painted the same garish blue as the camp buildings, only here the paint was in better shape, and someone had contrived blue and white embellishments of painted breeze blocks where the front garden had been. She thought perhaps the camp manager retired here, away from the worst of the jollifications, when his day's work was done. Whoever used it, it was now part of the abomination, and it set her teeth on edge as much as anything she had seen.

It was not until several miles farther on that she saw the bungalow. It was as much of an eyesore, in its way, as the holiday camp, but less intrusive. It just sat there, in the middle of that dark, tremendous landscape, looking as if it had been lifted bodily from the Brighton suburbs. She had seen bungalows like it in Cornwall and the wilder parts of Wales. Perhaps people saturated with natural beauty had no thought for the artificial, or perhaps the wildness of their surroundings drove them into the extremes of surburban cosiness. At any rate, give your Celtic outlier half a chance, and he would pull down the ancient stonework and put up a pebble-dashed horror like this.

The road dipped in a curve under it, and as Kate took the bend, she felt the steering go soggy in her hands and the car begin to jolt on the uneven tarmac. The bungalow, which she had damned at sight, became on the instant more acceptable. If there was one thing certain about a place like that, it was that someone lived in it, and if she was going to have a puncture on this road, she would much rather do it where there were people about. She was not the totally helpless woman driver who could only sit and wait for a man to come along. She knew what needed doing, and where the spare was and how the jack worked. But she had no great strength in her arms and hands, and mere intelligence was no match for a sticky wheel-nut. She pulled the limping car in to the side of the road and got out. It was a front tyre, and well down already. The silence, now she had stopped the engine, was absolute. Below the road the grey water lay among the stones as inert as oil. Above, the bungalow stared out blindly over it. Nothing moved anywhere. She went round to the back of the car and started to get the things out.

She worked the jack under the sagging corner of the car and managed to lift it before the wheel settled right down on its rims. So far so good. She had been taught that you must start the wheel nuts before the wheel was spinning free, but starting them was the thing she was not sure she could do. She levered the hub-cap off and fitted the brace over what looked, for no valid reason at all, the easiest nut. Then she turned and looked up at the bungalow.

It still showed no sign of life, but she had a strong feeling that there was someone there and that they were watching her. Well, if there was anyone there, they would be. She did not need telling that in a place like this the mere sound of a car would bring you to the window, whatever you were doing. She turned again, faintly resentful but obstinate, and began to wrestle with the nut. Almost to her surprise, she felt it move. She undid it a couple of turns and thought to hell with the bungalow. The second nut was harder, but gave when she got her foot on the crank of the brace. It was the third that beat her. She struggled with it, getting hot and angry, and hurting her hands in their driving gloves and even her right foot in its modestly towny shoe. She stopped and straightened herself, pushing her hair back off her forehead with the clean back of her glove. Something moved in the corner of her eye, and when she looked up at the bungalow, there was a woman standing just inside the gate, looking down at her.

The woman made no move. She looked quite young, several years younger than Kate. She had fair hair and a pale face, rather sharp and watchful. She did not look any more capable of shifting the wheel-nut than Kate was, but she could not be living here by herself. Anyhow, something must be done with her. They could not stand there looking at each other indefinitely, nor could Kate simply turn and resume her struggle with the nut, even if she thought it would do any good. She took off her gloves, made a bit more of a job of her hair and walked up the path towards the bungalow.

All the time the woman watched her. She looked neither friendly nor hostile, simply interested and non-committal. It was like the way the sleeping-car man and Alec had looked at her, but without the overtones of male superiority. When she got near enough, Kate smiled and the woman, very slightly, smiled back. She said, 'Is it a puncture you have?'

Kate nodded. 'I'm afraid so, yes. There's a nut I can't shift. I suppose your husband isn't at home?' The woman's hands were on the top of the gate, and she was near enough now to see the wedding-ring.

The woman said, 'No, he's away to Duncraigie. But he'll be back in a wee while. Or maybe the van'll be along. You'd best come in and wait.' She stood back and opened the gate.

'That's very kind of you,' said Kate. 'If I won't be a nuisance.'

'Oh, you'll no be a nuisance at all,' the woman said. She turned and led the way up the concrete path to the side door. She wore a jersey and tweed skirt, plain but solid and good, and, like all the people round here, she moved with style.

The kitchen was small but orderly and warm and full of electric gear. It had not yet occurred to Kate to marvel at the ubiquity of electric power in this empty world. Instead she found herself remembering what Mr Haskell had said the evening before. She wondered whether the woman would know she had not had any breakfast, and was ready, absurdly on the defensive, to explain that she never did. She shut the door after her, and the woman turned and said, 'You'd like a cup of coffee, maybe?'

It was perfectly ordinary and hospitable, but it came too pat on her thought. For a moment she hesitated, but this was ridiculous. She said again, 'That's very kind of you. Yes, I'd like one very much,' and the woman nodded and went to the stove.

Kate said, 'It's a quiet place you live in here.'

The woman turned and looked at her for a moment before she answered. 'Ay,' she said, 'it's quiet now, right enough. It's not so quiet when the camp is open. Then it's traffic on the road all the time, and the road was never meant for it. It was quiet all the time when the Colonel built the house for us. Six years ago, that will be. Then old Mr Macalister had his accident, and they were building the camp before the year was out. It's never been quiet since, not half the year.'

The woman had her back to her again, busy over the saucepan on the stove. Her voice was low but very clear, and Kate's ear was getting better attuned. It was only the names she found difficult now, and they were pure Gaelic and monstrously spelt. She said, 'I came past the camp just now. And an old house next to it that's been taken over too, by the look of it.'

The woman said, 'Ay, Mrs Cameron's house, that was. She left when the camp came.'

'She would,' said Kate. 'It's awful.'

'You think so?'

'Awful,' said Kate. Her mind was back with the old laird, as it had been earlier. She hesitated, and then, as the woman brought her coffee over and put it on the table in front of her, said half of what was in her mind. 'Old Mr Macalister,' she said. 'That would be Mr James Macalister's father, would it?'

The woman stood there, looking down at her as she sat at the table with her coffee. She said, 'Ay, just.'

Kate put a spoonful of castor sugar into her cup from a glass bowl on the table. It was powdered coffee out of a tin, and better sweetened. She said, 'He didn't want the camp?'

'Not he,' said the woman, 'not at any price. Forbye he needed the money, from what was said.'

Kate was committed now. She wanted the story, even if it meant cross-examining an uncommunicative witness. She looked up at the woman, and the woman looked down at her, still with the same steady, unwavering scrutiny. 'Then what?' said Kate. 'He died, I gather. Did you say he had an accident?'

The woman turned and went back to her stove. She picked up the empty saucepan and took it to the sink. She spoke, as she had before, without turning round. She said, 'He shot himself on the hill. It was an accident, they said.' There was nothing in it but the form of the words. The tone was still scrupulously neutral.

Kate said, 'And then Mr James sold out?'

'Ay,' said the woman, 'he was away south when it happened. But he was for selling, right enough.' Her eyes went to the window, and her face lightened. Kate saw or heard nothing outside, but a moment later the door opened and a man came in, treading softly in his rubber boots. He was as dark as his wife was fair, but had the same serious, sharpish face, as if he spent a lot of time listening to the silence. He checked when he saw Kate and pulled off his tweed cap. His eyes went to his wife for a moment and then came back to Kate. He gave her the same small, cautious smile. 'Hullo, there,' he said. It was not familiar at all, merely friendly and polite, but he looked at her as men did look at her.

The woman said, 'The lady has a puncture. She wonders can you help her with it?'

'Ay,' he said, 'I saw the car,' and Kate got up and took

up her gloves.

She said, 'There's a wheel-nut I can't shift. If you could just get it started —' She might be a lady, but she was determined not to be the helpless female.

'Of course,' he said. He stood there with his cap in his hand. The door was still open. Kate turned to the woman.

'I'm terribly grateful to you,' she said. 'That coffee made all the difference.'

'Oh, that's nothing. It's nice to see someone.' The smile was warmer now. The whole atmosphere was easier with the man's arrival.

Kate went to the door. 'I suppose it is,' she said. 'At this time of the year, anyhow. Well – goodbye, then. And thank you very much.'

The woman said, 'Goodbye, Mrs Wychett.'

Kate went down the concrete path, and the man put his cap on and followed her down. They would know who she was, of course. All the same, there was this feeling of living out in the open, where every movement showed. She supposed she would get used to it, but it made her uneasy.

When they came to the car, the man went straight to it and got his hands on the brace. They were small, neat hands, but strong and workmanlike. He heaved on the brace. She hoped it would not move too easily, and it did not. He said, 'It's stuck, right enough.'

Kate said, 'I managed the first two, but I couldn't shift this one.' She was still slightly on the defensive, but the man gave her a quick sideways smile before he turned back to the brace.

'You would not,' he said. 'Don't you worry. We'll shift it.' He held the brace on the nut with both hands and put his foot on the crank. The heavy rubber boot came down with a cushioned force well beyond the reach of her leather shoe, and at the second kick the crank turned. 'There she is,' he said. 'We'll no be long now.'

'That's wonderful,' said Kate. She no longer felt spiky, merely pleased to have the man helping her. 'If you wouldn't mind just starting the other nut. I haven't tried that yet. But once it's started, I can do the rest.' She knew she would feel a little put out if he took her at her word, but he did not.

He said again, 'Oh, don't you worry. There's no call for you to get yourself messed with it.' He looked at her again, taking in her indefeasible elegance, but now she did not mind. She stood there watching him while he got on with the job. He worked with the calculated deliberation of a man not used to working against the clock, but he wasted no time.

When the spare was on and the flat put away in the back of the car, he said, 'You'll be going into Aberwhinnie?'

'Yes,' she said, 'but I've only got shopping to do. It's nothing urgent.'

'Ay,' he said. 'Just so. You'll want to get the flat mended before you come home. It's not a road to be on without a spare. Jimmy Brown will do it for you. On the right where the first houses are. You'll see the pumps. You'd best leave it with him as you go in.'

She said, 'Oh yes, thank you. I'll do that.' She got into the driving seat, and he stood there by the side of the car. She no longer felt on her guard with him. She said, 'Your wife was telling me about old Mr Macalister. His death, I mean. I was asking her about the holiday camp.'

'Ay,' he said. It was not decisively a question, but it told her nothing. He just stood there, looking down at her, and waiting for her to say what she wanted to say. She did not want to go on now. She worried even herself by the extent of her interest, and her instinct, now that it was too late, was to conceal it. She looked up into his thin, serious face, begging him mentally to let her off the hook. When he did speak, what he said did not make it any better. He said, 'You'll likely be interested.'

Once again, it was not so much a question as a sort of tentative statement, offered for her rejection if she did not like it. She took her eyes off his and busied herself with the car. She said, 'I don't know – it just seemed sad coming when it did. I mean – if it hadn't happened just then, they'd probably have taken their beastly camp somewhere else.' She started the engine and put the gears into first.

The man nodded. 'Maybe,' he said. 'It was a bad business, right enough. But he was an old man, and things weren't well with him. And they were all on to him about selling. Maybe he was plain sick of the whole business.'

'You mean you think it wasn't an accident?'

He shrugged. 'That there's no saying,' he said. 'Yon Alec, he said it was an accident, and there was nothing to show to the contrary. If it had been some of those that come up for the stalking, now, I'd not say but what it might have been. But Mr Macalister was near born with a rifle in his hand.' He looked up at the dark sky, and Kate, sitting in the car, saw suddenly that it had started to rain.

She said, 'You mustn't get wet. Thank you very much. And please thank your wife again for me.'

'It's a pleasure,' he said. She let in the clutch and moved off, leaving him standing there by the roadside. She felt a sudden enormous distaste for the whole place, but she knew it would not do. Richard was happy here, and she was stuck with it. She must get the flat tyre mended and do her shopping and get back to the school.

But even at the school there was Mrs Haskell. It was not that there were too many people. There were too few, and not enough for them to think about except each other. The great thing was not to get involved. She had her own life to lead. But she knew that she was, in spite of herself, involved already, and she did not like it.

The rain came down in a soft, persistent drizzle, and she had lost just the wrong amount of time. She might still get back for lunch if she hurried, but she did not want to hurry on that road, even with the spare tyre safely mended. Nor, on the other hand, did she want to get herself lunch in Aberwhinnie. In the end she bought a couple of sausage rolls to eat as she drove, but they were greasy and unappetising, and there was little sustenance in them. She drove back carefully, but oppressed by a wholly unreasonable sense of guilt and urgency. She got back to the house a little before two and found Richard still at home, with the remains of a scratch lunch on the kitchen table.

'I'm so sorry,' she said. 'I got a puncture and had to wait for help. One of the wheel-nuts was jammed. Why didn't you get a proper lunch at the school? You said you could.'

He was placid and full of reassurance, so that it was a comfort to have him there. 'So I could,' he said. 'But I found I had got the last hour free, and I thought you might be back. Anyway, it was just as easy to get myself something here. What about you? Have you had anything?'

'Not really. Only a rather horrible snack. I'll get myself something now.'

'You do that. I've got to get back to the school, anyway, so take your time.'

He gathered his things together and went to the door. 'Oh, by the way,' he said, 'Macalister called. He's asked us to dine with him.'

'Called here? What time was that, then?'

'I don't know. A bit after twelve, I suppose. It was only a chance I was here. Anyway, I accepted for Wednesday. Will that be all right?'

'Fine, I should think. I'll be interested to see how he does us.'

He smiled. 'Not trifle, anyway, I hope. See you later.'

'Yes,' she said, 'all right.' The door shut on him, and she went into the kitchen. She felt slightly breathless. 'And be damned to you, Mr Macalister,' she said, but she knew as she said it that the defiance rang a little hollow.

VI

She made herself a plain omelette, and ate it slowly and resolutely. She did not feel hungry, but she knew she must be, and she wanted to bury the greasy memory of the sausage rolls. When she had finished, she washed up and put away the remains of Richard's meal and her own. Then she went into the sitting-room and tried to make up her mind what to do. She knew that the best thing she could do was to go out for a walk, like Prospero, to still her beating mind. But Prospero had had the balmy island air to walk in, and here the skies were dark and sullen, and the rain fell steadily. She felt nerveless and exhausted, and the thought of making herself waterproof all over again was too much for her. She switched on the electric fire for comfort, though the room was warm enough without it. She sat down, staring into the glow of the single bar, and knew at once that if she sat for long enough, she would go to sleep. It would be the easy way out, but she suspected that she would feel even worse when she woke up. All the same, her eyelids began to droop.

The ring was startlingly peremptory and brought her guiltily to her feet. For some reason, when everything else was electric, they had fitted doorbells of the kind you ring by turning a knob on the outside of the door, so that the quality of the ring reflected the amount of energy you put into it. It may have been only to her drowsy mind that it sounded so urgent. She hurried out into the hall. She did not reach the point of telling herself consciously that it was James Macalister, but she knew afterwards that the thought had been there. It was Mrs Haskell.

She was waterproofed, of course, with a hood covering her hair and framing her face, but she was not dressed for a cross-country walk. The shoes were solid enough, but probably only what she wore all day. She stood there, looking at Kate out of her hood with a curious mixture of determination and diffidence. Kate was not glad to see her at all, but felt guilty that she was not. She did not like Mrs Haskell, but was disconcerted to find that she felt sorry for her. 'Hullo,' she said. 'Come in.' It was on the tip of her tongue to say 'I wondered who it was', but she did not say it.

'May I? I was up this way, and I hoped you might be at home.' She took off her mackintosh and hood, and stood there with the wet things in her hands, wondering what to do with them.

'Give those to me,' said Kate. She hung them on a hook at the side of the hall, where they could drip harmlessly on the tiles.

'Oh,' said Mrs Haskell. 'Yes. Thank you. If that will be all right.' She seemed as awkward as a child, but her awkwardness was conscious and faintly defiant, as if she was daring you to see anything wrong with it.

Kate waved her towards the open door of the sitting-room and followed her in. 'Come in,' she said. 'I'd just switched the fire on. It's a miserable afternoon.' She switched on a light for good measure, and shut the door behind her.

Mrs Haskell stood in the middle of the room, looking round at its austere elegance, so unlike the uninformed austerity of her own. 'You've got settled in,' she said. There was little of the Highlands in her speech, but she had this same trick of using an affirmative form of words for what seemed at least half a question. And she was appraising, thought Kate, always appraising, looking to see what you were at and setting her own valuation on it.

'Oh yes,' said Kate. 'It's a nice little house, and beautifully warm.' She wished at once that she had left out the 'little'. It suggested comparisons, a comparison with some mansion she might have left behind her in the south, or with Mrs Haskell's own house, which was a good deal bigger. Comparisons were a thing which, with Mrs Haskell, you avoided at all costs. She did not think the point had been missed, but she said, 'Do sit down', before anything could be made of it. 'Would you like some tea?' she said. 'It's a bit early, but it might be rather nice.' It annoyed her that she felt bound to justify the suggestion, as if anticipating Mrs Haskell's disapproval.

Mrs Haskell said, 'Oh. Well, yes, if you're making it anyhow.' She did not quite look at her watch, but made no attempt to dissemble her faint surprise.

'Good,' said Kate. 'I'll put the kettle on.' When she came back, Mrs Haskell still sat there, motionless and straight-backed. She had not wandered about the room looking at things, and she was not now ready with comment or suggestion. She just sat there, taking it all in and thinking her own thoughts.

It was over the tea that she said suddenly, 'I see you've had visitors.' She said it, not looking at Kate, as if it was forced out of her. She was slightly flushed.

For a moment Kate genuinely did not know what she meant. 'Visitors?' she said. Then she understood, and wished passionately that she had not asked the question. To Mrs Haskell she knew it would sound prevaricating and disingenuous, and she covered it quickly. 'Oh, you mean Mr Macalister?' she said. She said it calmly, but she was appalled by the violence of her feelings and confused by their complication. There was anger certainly, but also there was a sort of instinctive recoil, an enormous distaste for the manner and motivation of Mrs Haskell's inquiry. She was still in some part of her mind sorry for her, but she found her nasty and even a little frightening. Richard had said straight away that she was dangerous, and he was not one to over-estimate people. For herself, she did not see where the danger could lie, but she felt the malice as palpably as a cold draught.

Mrs Haskell was looking at her now, with a hard, direct stare. 'I saw his car in the drive,' she said, 'and it would not be – anyone else he was coming to see.'

There was a minute hesitation before the 'anyone else'. She nearly said 'us', thought Kate. It might even have been 'me'. She said, 'That's right. Richard saw him. I was out at Aberwhinnie.'

Mrs Haskell nodded and looked away. There was a moment's silence. Then she picked up her cup and drank. 'I don't like the man,' she said.

Kate had recovered herself now, and was armed at all points. She spoke with studied lightness. 'No?' she said. 'Well, I hardly know him, of course.' She hoped desperately that the subject was closed, but it was not.

'There was a Mrs Burnley here. Her husband was on John's staff. He was for ever hanging around her. Everybody was talking about it.'

Kate said, 'That I don't doubt.'

Mrs Haskell was looking at her again now. 'The man is a plain philanderer,' she said.

Kate managed a small laugh. It did not sound very convincing, even to her, but she managed it. 'Oh well,' she said, 'I don't expect you or I are in much danger from his dishonourable attentions.'

'I?' said Mrs Haskell. 'He would not dare try it on with the headmaster's wife.'

She looked away again, and Kate looked at her sitting there, bolt upright and somehow out of place in that pleasant room. There was nothing wrong with her physically. She was a healthy young woman, with a large, splendid body and a clear skin, though the skin was naturally highly coloured and untouched by art. Even the face, under that tightly coiled auburn hair, was correctly shaped, if on the same scale as the rest of her. But it had no grace in its looks. It was the mind that was wrong. She wondered what it would be like being married to a woman like that. She tried to imagine the civilised, capable John Haskell in bed with his Janet. Her mind could not or would not construct the picture, but it sensed ugly disparities. She wanted badly to change the subject, but she was not sure she would be allowed to, nor could she think of anything else she could talk convincingly to Mrs Haskell about. She tried a partial diversion. She said, 'I saw the holiday camp this morning. I must say, it is a bit of an eyesore.'

'It is an abomination.' Her voice shook a little, and Kate saw suddenly that she meant exactly what she said. Abomination was one of the devalued words. No one now used it wholly seriously. Mrs Haskell did, so that there was the reek of hell-fire in it. She set her mouth again, and looked at Kate. 'And to think he's making money out of it.'

Kate looked at her, hoping against hope that she would smile, but she was unaware of the bathos. There was something Mr Haskell had said about the sensibility of the glen's honour and its pocket. That was not quite right. She did not suppose Mrs Haskell herself stood to lose anything from the camp. It was just that her malice fed wherever it could find anything to feed on. There was no nicety in malice, and certainly no humour. She gave up any thought of subtlety herself, and put down the ground-bait with a heavy hand. She said, 'I expect he needed the money. And then the offer was still open when old Mr Macalister died, so he took it.'

'Oh yes, trust him. Accidental death, they said it was. A very convenient accident for Master James, if you ask me.'

Kate said, 'But Mr Macalister wasn't even here when it happened.'

Mrs Haskell looked at her, and suddenly and unnervingly smiled. She said, 'You're well up on the facts, I see. But that Alec was here.'

That Alec, thought Kate. Yon Alec, the man in the bungalow had said. Mrs Haskell's was only an English translation. Alec with his almost animal silence and the drink lines round his mouth. But the thing had gone far enough. She was desperate to get rid of Mrs Haskell now, but did not know how to set about it. She did not think she would be susceptible to ordinary pressures. She put her cup down decisively and got to her feet. She said, 'Really, Mrs Haskell, I don't know whether to take you seriously or not, but this does seem to me a very dangerous way to talk. I'm new here. Mr Macalister's affairs are no concern of mine, and I don't intend that they shall be. Please can't we leave it at that?'

Mrs. Haskell got up too, but slowly. She seemed once more completely at a loss, as if she recognised the force of the outburst, but could not properly account for it. She even smiled slightly, but Kate could not make out whether the smile was placatory or derisive. The words, when they came, seemed meant to be disarming, but she still did not like the quality of the smile. 'Oh, there now,' said Mrs Haskell, 'I've upset you, and I was minded only to help you.' The Highland speech was suddenly very much more pronounced, as if she was taking refuge in her foreignness, or even asserting a sort of privilege in it. Kate knew, almost to the letter, what was coming next, and knew, this time, how she would deal with it. 'It will be strange to you here,' said Mrs Haskell, 'but you'll get used to our ways.'

Kate said, 'You're mistaken, Mrs Haskell. I married an Englishman, as you did, but my father was a Macinnes. I'm as Scottish as you are.'

She hoped at least that she would not be cross-examined on her credentials, but she was altogether unprepared for the effect her claim produced. Mrs Haskell spun round to face her. Her eyes were wide and her face suddenly flooded with colour. 'You are?' she said. She seemed completely disconcerted and in some way almost mortified. 'I had not heard that,' she said.

'Well, really,' said Kate, 'I don't know why you should,' but she knew well enough. Mrs Haskell's intelligence system had let her down, and she was not used to it. She led the way out into the hall, and Mrs Haskell came with her. She helped her on with her waterproofs. Neither of them said anything, but the moral advantage of the silence was all Kate's.

It was still raining outside. Mrs Haskell pulled her hood over her head and turned on the doorstep. She had the same look now as she had had when she came in, uncertain but determined. She said, 'You'll come and see me some time, perhaps? We're so close.'

For a moment Kate thought she was going to suggest a day and time. She searched desperately in her mind for excuses, but knew she had none. She did not consciously hesitate, but Mrs Haskell, still peering at her out of her hood, came in again before she could answer. This time the Highland touch seemed unconscious. 'Oh, any time,' she said. 'I'm mostly at home, you'll find. For now I must be away. Goodbye, Mrs Wychett.'

She turned and went off down the path under the dark drizzle. Kate said 'Goodbye' to her vanishing back. Then she shut the door, and turned and leant her back against it, as if to make sure that she kept it shut and saw nothing but the inside of her own home. She stayed there, breathing deeply and quietly, until she felt the wood of the door strike cool on the back of her head through the hair. Then she went into the sitting-room and gathered up the tea things. She took them into the kitchen and washed them up and put them away. She went back into the sitting-room and made sure that everything was exactly as it had been before Mrs Haskell had come in. She wanted no trace of her presence left. But the fire was no good to her now. She did not want to sit, let alone sleep. She turned it off and went and put on waterproofs and boots.

When she got outside, the afternoon seemed darker than ever, but the rain had almost stopped. The air was full of a drifting watery vapour, but it condensed only intermittently into palpable drops. She walked quickly down the hill and turned off on a side path which went in a sweep round the back of the Haskells' house and brought her out on the drive near the main gate. Once she was out on the road beyond the river and the school buildings, she was out of sight of the staff houses. From the Haskells' house even the skyline on the other side of the glen was invisible. She had gone to some trouble already to be sure of this.

But she was climbing no hill-faces today. Instead she turned eastwards and set off briskly along the road. It was exercise she needed now, not adventure. She walked steadily for nearly half an hour, hearing nothing but the soft thud of her boots on the tarmac and the murmur of the river. She came to no conclusion at all, because there was none to come to, but she was conscious of a lightening of the spirit. When she decided she had gone far enough, she turned off the road and sat down on a rock under the steep face of the hill. There seemed to be more light at the bottom of the glen than there was higher up, as if the river water and the wet tarmac were somehow carrying it through the tunnel of the dark hills and the lowering sky. She felt utterly alone and therefore safe. There was no menace in the place itself. Perhaps there was something after all in this business of Highland blood, so that to her at least this huge cloudy landscape spoke nothing but peace. The threat was in the people. Now she would go home and tell Richard about Mrs Haskell's visit.

She got up from her rock and began to walk slowly back to the road. She was half-way there when she heard a shot up on the hill behind her. She stopped on the instant, and a moment later there was a second shot. Two shots, no more. The silence settled in again, but now there was no peace in it. There was only one person who would be shooting up there, and one person who would be with him. Two men up on the hill and now, she supposed, one dead beast, that had needed two bullets before it died. She went back to the road and set out for home, almost running in her agitation. She did not want to face the dark house without Richard, but she reckoned that however fast she went, he would be back before her.

She saw the lights before she came to the house, and as she opened the door she heard Richard in the kitchen whistling peacefully above the gentle clatter of china. She got rid of her waterproofs and went through to join him. He looked up, smiled at her and turned back to the kettle. 'Hullo,' he said, 'had a good walk?'

'Yes,' she said. 'I didn't go far. Just along the road.'

He looked at her again, kindly and detached, and she looked back at him, and time passed, and she said nothing more. Then he nodded and said, 'Good,' and the time was gone for ever.

VII

She had her hair done in Aberwhinnie on the Wednesday morning, and was pleasantly surprised at the result. The girl was competent in a placid, unhurried sort of way, as the man in the bungalow had been with her wheel. This was a perfectly normal procedure. You had your hair done at regular intervals anyway, and naturally you took occasion to have it done before any sort of a party. She assumed that Richard, if he noticed these things at all, would take it for granted. The only unusual thing was the fact that it occurred to her to wonder if he would. She was back long before he got in, and when he did, she asked him about clothes.

'Well,' he said, 'I'm wearing a black tie. Macalister said would I mind, and I said of course not. So you know what you're up against.'

Kate was suddenly and unexpectedly pleased. She liked dressing up. 'Oh good,' she said.

'Yes. I'm all for the proper touches in a suitably feudal setting. So long as we don't have pipers behind our chairs. I couldn't hear what was being said.'

She laughed cheerfully. 'I don't see the laird going to those lengths,' she said. 'I don't think his feudality would go beyond his comforts. He wouldn't want to call the tune if it meant paying the piper.'

He looked at her, glad of her cheerfulness and interested in her critical assessment. 'You're probably right,' he said. 'Let's hope he pays his cook instead. I'm glad there's some civilisation in the glen, I must say. I was afraid you were going to find the social side a bit bleak.'

She was on the defensive again now, slightly irritated but

determined not to show it. She said, 'I'm not pining for the bright lights, I assure you. But I agree with you. It's nice dining properly if one's going to dine at all.'

They left it at that, but it gave her the excuse she wanted to put in a little extra work on herself. She went to get ready early, and picked with a clear conscience a rather dashing little dark red she had hardly hoped to be able to wear up here. When she was almost ready, Richard came in and stood behind her, looking her over in the glass. 'Coo,' he said. 'No tartan sash?'

She smiled back at him in the glass. He looked as if he had been born in a dinner jacket. She said, 'From what I remember, the Macinnes tartan wouldn't go.'

'A pity. You'll have to get yourself a kilt for less formal occasions.'

'A skirt,' she said. 'Women don't wear the kilt, just a pleated skirt. As discreet as the kilt is not.'

'Never mind,' he said. 'Perhaps Macalister will wear the kilt.'

He did not, in fact, but the other man did, and the effect was breath-taking. To complete Kate's pleasure, the man's wife wore black, a tasteful foil to her husband's brilliance, but not in the same class as Kate's dark red. They were a Colonel and Mrs Grant, fiftyish or thereabouts, from somewhere along the glen. Despite the Highland trappings, everybody spoke standard southern English. And after all, thought Kate, why not? It was a long time now since the queen's favourite courtier had spoken broad West Country, and nationalism could not be expected to override class. Anecdotally, if they wanted it, they all had the local speech at their fingers' ends, but they would not speak it among themselves, or even to those who did.

The meal was unpretentious but pleasant, and the company were on good terms with themselves and each other. James Macalister was so good a host that you did not notice his being one. He did not, as Jane Austen would have said, distinguish Kate at all, but she knew he was aware of her, and she was constantly and almost painfully aware of him. Behind the social glow and the geniality of alcohol her mind sat back and took stock of the situation. Richard, to start with, was enjoying himself. Whether he knew what was happening to her she did not know, but it would not be James Macalister's fault if he did, nor, she hoped, her own. That it was happening was as unarguable as the weather and apparently as unavoidable. She had never to her knowledge felt like this before, but it was all immediately familiar and natural. Its naturalness was the most extraordinary thing about it. Here was something which, if she was not very careful, could blow her whole life to pieces, and it came as naturally as breathing. That was what made it so appallingly difficult to be careful. Her mind seemed to be working, with perfect clarity, on three different levels. There was the social level, on which she found herself dealing with Richard along with the rest. There was the secret level, on which she swam luxuriously in a sort of radiant glow of unimaginable pleasure. And below both these, somewhere down in the pit of her well-fed stomach, there was, never wholly hidden from her, a cold and bottomless apprehension.

When she and Mrs Grant withdrew, she left Richard to James Macalister with no shadow of anxiety, but with Mrs Grant she was, for all the pleasantness, immediately on her guard. You had to be with women, far more than with men. There was a picture in the hall as they went through towards the drawing-room, a portrait she had not noticed before. It was a commanding figure in Highland dress. As such, so far as she was concerned, it was dateless, but the picture did not look old. She stopped to look at it, and Mrs Grant stopped with her. She said, 'James's father. Some time back, of course.'

Despite the bright colours and the splendid stance, it was the face that held her. It was not a nice face. Whoever had painted the thing, he had gone to town on his picture, but he had been honest with his subject. The green eyes were hard and watchful and the mouth a little thin. There was none of his son's easy geniality about the old laird. She said, 'So that's him. I'm always hearing him spoken of.'

'Oh yes,' said Mrs Grant, 'a great local figure in his day.'

Kate looked at her and saw she was smiling slightly. She said, 'Yes. Yes, so I gather.' She looked at the picture again.

Mrs Grant said, 'Not much likeness, is there?'

'To James?' She hesitated, with something nagging at the back of her mind. 'No,' she said, 'I don't think so. There's a sort of reminiscence somewhere, but I can't put my finger on it.'

They went on into the drawing-room. Mrs Grant said, 'James will be like his mother, I imagine. I don't remember her. She died a long time back. I can't say I cared awfully for the old man myself, but he was God Almighty in the glen. James didn't get on with him, of course.'

Kate said, 'Interesting,' and Mrs Grant looked at her questioningly. 'I mean,' she said, 'interesting the different views you get of people.'

'Oh, that,' said Mrs Grant. 'You'll get used to that.' She paused, looking Kate over. 'James tells me you're a Macinnes,' she said.

A red light came on and glowed faintly in Kate's mind. Then she remembered that she had already told Mrs Haskell. The thing could be common knowledge by now, anyhow. 'Well, yes,' she said, 'but not really a card-carrying member. I was born in Bombay.'

'My dear, we all were. I don't mean Bombay necessarily, but England or somewhere. The diaspora was nothing to what's happened to us. But it doesn't do any harm to carry your card now you're here. You look the part, anyhow. I agree it's no good making a thing of it further south. The sort of man who wears the kilt in Jermyn Street only makes us all look silly.'

The middle level of Kate's mind suddenly threw up a perfectly clear picture of her changing the Macinnes tartan for the Macalister and settling down in the glen to breed, among others, a new little laird. It was a meltingly warm picture, which the rest of her mind stared at for a moment with a sort of horrified incredulity. She spoke to Mrs Grant without any apparent pause. She said, 'That would have been my father, more or less. I don't mean I ever actually saw him do it, but he was like that, and I'm afraid I reacted pretty violently against it. Of course, when we knew we were coming up here, Richard pulled my leg about my Highland blood stirring, but I wouldn't hear of it.'

Mrs Grant looked at her, smiling. 'Well,' she said, 'I won't ask if it has, because you would probably be at pains to deny it. Your Richard is the obstacle, of course. The nicest type of Englishman, the sort we are all really in bondage to, whatever we say about the Westminster parliament and the redcoats. You'll have to compromise. That's what we all do, after all.'

'Yes,' said Kate, 'I expect so.' It only occurred to her afterwards that on her stated position there was nothing to compromise with. She wondered whether it had occurred to Mrs Grant too. As for the secret part of her, she knew that to talk of compromise was only an evasion. What she wanted was the best of both worlds. To have her cake and eat it. A graceless, undignified expression, she thought, especially to anyone as hungry as she was. When the men came in, Richard was still evidently in high good humour, and she looked at him as if she had never seen him before in her life.

She looked at Colonel Grant, too, a sight for sore eyes in his pleats and buckles and bunches of lace, courteous, deferential, very slightly sardonic, altogether out of reach. She did not look at James Macalister at all, except as one of the company. She knew him already by heart. Everybody continued to behave admirably. It was a most successful evening altogether.

It was only at the end, when he was helping her into her coat, that they were out of earshot of the rest. He said, 'Good night, Catriona,' and she said, 'Good night, James,' as if there was nothing in it. Then she went out with Richard to the car.

The feeling of unfamiliarity struck her again with startling force. She had left the warmth and light and the company she knew, and found herself alone in the dark with a stranger. They spoke to each other as they always spoke, but it was like using words picked out of a foreign-language phrase-book. You were never quite sure what the other person really understood by what you said. Richard said, 'You've got to hand it to our James. He does things very well. Didn't you think so?'

'Yes,' said Kate, 'I enjoyed it enormously. I liked Mrs Grant. I couldn't make much of the Colonel.'

'I dare say not. Not really a squire of dames, despite the peacock plumes. But highly intelligent in a hard-bitten sort of way. Very much the professional soldier. I've met plenty like him. And I must say, I like the laird, holiday camp or no holiday camp.'

Kate said, 'Did you see his father?'

He turned for a moment and looked at her. 'Did I —?'

'In the hall. On your left as you went towards the dining-room. Full length in glorious Technicolor.'

'Good lord, was that the old laird? I thought it was an ancestor. The dress, of course. I didn't look at him properly. A bit fishy-eyed, from what I remember.'

'Yes. Not very prepossessing. Mrs Grant obviously didn't like him. She said he and James didn't get on.' The name came easily. The context was just right, of course.

Richard nodded without taking his eyes off the road. 'Interesting,' he said. 'And the glen sees him as the grand old man. Or perhaps that's only Janet. I must sound out Haskell on him.'

Kate said, 'Does it matter?' and he turned and looked at her again.

'Not in the least,' he said cheerfully. 'But reputations are interesting things, especially to a historian. The laird in his glen, the monarch in his kingdom. A sort of microcosm. And the evidence just as biased and contradictory.'

'It frightens me a bit. There's too much of it. I don't want to get involved.'

He said, 'Lord bless you, why should you?' and they drove in silence until he swung the car into the school gates. There were not many lights now, but in the headmaster's house they still showed behind the heavy curtains downstairs. Richard said, 'Janet sitting up for us, I shouldn't wonder,' and Kate shivered suddenly inside her coat, but he did not notice.

She knew that they would make love before they went to sleep. They always did after a party, and she wanted it. It was all a part of the state she was in over James Macalister, but she did not pretend that there was any logic in this. The moral issue, if there was one, she did not even examine. She and Richard would make love, when they were both undressed and washed and ready for bed, and it would take some of the steam out of her. Only no dreams afterwards, she thought, please God no dreams. Let me make love and sleep, and in the morning I will look at the whole thing all over again from the beginning.

Just before they went to sleep, when they were both back in their own beds, Richard said, 'You know, I think you'd better get that skirt. The tartan, I mean.'

'Why?'

'I don't know. I think there's something in it. Now you're up here, I mean. It seems a pity to turn your back on history.'

'That's what Mrs Grant said, more or less.'

'Did she? She would, I suppose. I find it very interesting and rather attractive. Anyway, think about it.'

She said, 'All right.' Something else to think about in the morning. Then they did sleep, and this time there were no dreams at all.

It was Kate who woke first. They never used an alarm, even on working mornings. One or the other of them always woke early enough, and when the time came to make the tea, whoever was awake made it. There was no explicit agreement about it and nothing for anyone to feel guilty or aggrieved about. It just worked like that. When Kate woke, she had already made up her mind. There was twenty minutes or so to go before she need make the tea and she lay quiet, thinking over what she had to do and even re-hearsing details. The main decision was made. She must see James and tell him that the thing could not go on and why. That the thing was there, and that they both knew it was there, she had no doubt at all, even though nothing had been said. Obviously, she did not know James's side of it as well as she knew her own, but that did not matter, because it was going no further anyhow. But she could not leave the thing implicit and unacknowledged. She and James must say, once, what they had to say to each other. Once it was said, they would both be able to leave it, as it would always be, between them, because there was nothing else they could do. She did not doubt their ability to do this, but they must both know what they were doing. She would make occasion to see him. She was not sure when or how. Perhaps she would telephone. But see him she must.

She looked across at Richard. He was still asleep. He slept as he behaved awake, neatly and quietly and in perfect taste. She felt as remote from him as ever, but perfectly friendly now, because the thing was settled and her conscience was clear. She got out of bed and put on her dressing-gown and went to make the tea. When she came back with the tray, Richard was awake. He lay comfortably on his back, as she had lain, staring at the ceiling. She did not know what he was thinking about at all. He turned his head sideways on the pillow and looked at her. For a moment he considered her, as if he was trying to fit her into whatever it was he had been thinking about. Then he smiled. He said, 'The weather's cleared, thank God.' They never said good morning to each other, any more than they said good night, and the fact that she had made the tea did not need mentioning.

She said, 'Yes, it looks marvellous.' It occurred to her, as she said it, that she had not up to then noticed the weather at all.

She wondered if he would talk about the evening before, but instead he said, 'I think I've got a historian. Possibly two. A Level stuff. I'm going to have a word with Haskell about them.'

'Oh?' she said. 'Good.'

'Yes. It adds interest, certainly. The fact that they don't come here as examination fodder doesn't necessarily mean that they're all numbskulls. And of course the fact that the school doesn't get in a sweat over examinations doesn't necessarily mean that they wouldn't like getting a few results. Or so I imagine.'

She said, 'No, I'm sure you're right.' She was wondering, now that the world was moving about her again, whether she would really, when it came to the point, be able to telephone James. Perhaps she could ring up to thank him, politely, for a pleasant evening. That was perfectly in order. The great thing was to get in touch with him. She gave Richard the cup of tea she had been pouring out for him. It was exactly as he liked it. He rolled over and sat up in bed before he took it from her.

She poured out her own cup separately, because she liked it quite different. Then she said, 'Touch wood and so on, but the thing's working out, isn't it?'

He leant back, propped up on the pillows and sipping his tea very deliberately. 'I think so,' he said. 'I hope so, anyhow. At least, I don't see why it shouldn't. Do you?'

For a moment they looked at each other. Then she lifted her cup and drank. As she put it down, she shook her head. 'None at all,' she said. This was true, because the thing was settled. But she was in a hurry now to settle it, not only in her own mind, but with James. Until then, her answer was only provisionally true. That was all right, but it could not be left like that.

VIII

It was only when she got well up on to the hill that Kate saw the cloud to the south. Overhead the sky was still a washed-out blue, and as far as she could see the moor was a mixture of browns and yellows just streaked with green. It looked like a very discreet tweed. There was no wind at all. Even in the southern sky, where the cloud was, there was no sign of disturbance. Whatever was moving it, the cloud was not broken at all. It just hung there in a solid bank, its top level as a table. Above it, the sun still climbed in its flat autumnal curve, but the cloud was catching up with it. She thought it would be raining again before she got home, but she was dressed for it. She turned her back on the sun and the cloud and went on up the path.

She went on because she was committed to it, but she was frightened. She was frightened because she was committed and could not see what might come of it. But mainly she was afraid that she was making a fool of herself. Her deeper and more rational fears were concerned with Richard and her marriage and the hostile intelligences of the glen. The other fear was concerned only with James Macalister. It was irrational and unworthy, but it blanketed all the rest.

She hated telephones. She could never completely persuade herself that the person at the other end was really the person she thought she was talking to, or that the words divorced from the speaking face really meant what they said. James had said, 'Yes,' and then stopped. That was when she had got over the polite formalities and said she wanted to talk to him. He had stopped for so long that she had nearly yielded to panic and rushed into further explanations. Finally she had said 'James?' and he had said 'Yes. Yes, I'm thinking.' His voice had been perfectly level, as if he really was doing just that. Then he had said, 'I'll be up the Corrie Dorcha this morning. Do you think you could meet me there?' He had told her where it was. It did not sound too far or too difficult. She had said, 'All right. What about Alec?' and he had said, 'I'll be alone, of course.' She could not remember, now, exactly how the conversation had been broken off. It was the level tone that had upset her, and was still upsetting her. She had telephoned him with her heart in her mouth, and he had made the assignation like a man making a business appointment. And yet what in God's name did she expect or want? To talk to him, after all. To meet him and talk to him where they could not be seen or overheard, and to tell him what she felt and what she had decided. She went on up the path, and as she went the cloud shadow came up the path behind her and the whole world went suddenly dark.

This must be the beginning of the corrie, because the hill-faces were closing in on both sides, and the burn, which had been away to her left, was now almost under the path. It ran strongly between its boulders after the recent rains, and the noise it made filled the vast silence of the moor. But she must still be some way below the place she was making for. She did not turn round any more. There was nothing behind her but the moving cloud, and she knew about that. The path was steeper now, and she got a little out of breath as she hurried up it. The place had sounded fairly unmistakable. The burn forked where a side stream came in from the west, and just below the fork a single big black rock stood up over the path, so that the path jinked round its foot. James would be coming down the east side of the corrie, by a path which joined the southern path at the rock. The rock had a name, but she had not got hold of its Gaelic complexities. Whichever of them got there first was to wait until the other came. There must be no wandering about in the corrie. He had been very emphatic about that. Up the path to the black rock, and if he was not there, wait until he came. But he thought he would be.

Mostly she kept her eyes down on the rough going, but every now and then she looked up ahead of her, hoping to see the rock. She had still not seen it when she saw whisps of mist on the path ahead and the outline of the hilltops already blurred. It was very dark, as dark as it could be at that time of day. She was a little desperate now, and almost running, so that when it happened she could hardly stop herself. The light changed suddenly from a leaden dusk to a luminous phosphorescent grey, but now there was nothing to see. The world contracted in an instant to a few yards of broken ground under her feet. Beyond that and everywhere above it there was nothing but the seething mist. The voice of the burn went on. It seemed louder than ever, but she could not see where it came from. It was not only the shadow of the cloud-bank that had caught up with her now. It was the cloud itself.

She stopped and stood there, utterly at a loss and for a moment uncomfortably near to panic. If she had been afraid of the place, she might have panicked, with the pure primitive fear of the surrounding emptiness. But she had come to terms with the place. However obstinately she denied it, the place was in her blood. It was the more mundane, human complications she was afraid of, missing James, getting lost, getting back late, perhaps being looked for and involved in explanations. But even this was unreasonable. She did not have to account for her movements, still less for the movements of the clouds. It was only her guilt that gnawed at her, and she had come out to exorcise her guilt. She could still see the path. She gathered her waterproofs closer against the clinging damp and went on up it.

It was slower going now, and she was conscious of time passing. She breathed short and quick, but it was apprehension that shortened her breath, not exertion. She went on doggedly, telling herself that there could not be much farther to go. The voice came a minute or two later. It came out of the mist straight ahead of her. 'Catriona! Catriona!' It was a long-drawn, almost wailing shout, as if the voice was pitched deliberately through cupped hands.

Comfort and reassurance welled up in her, more unnerving than the preceding apprehension. She called, 'James! James! I'm here. I'm coming.' She almost broke into a run, stumbled on the uneven path, pulled herself back to a walk and saw almost at once the huge black shape of the rock and the smaller, paler shape of the man who stood under it. She called 'James!' again, and a moment later he was holding her by her arms.

He did not put his arms round her or bring her body against his. His hands took hold of the upper part of her arms, and he held her there, not quite at arm's length. She had come up to him with hands outstretched, but now under that compulsive grip they fell to her sides, and she stood there, head back, passive and limp, while he stared down at her and she stared up at him. He said, 'All right?' and she nodded. 'If you ever really get lost,' he said, 'go downhill. Go very carefully, but go downhill, and when you come to a burn, follow it. There's nearly always firm going along the side of a burn, if you go carefully, and any burn will take you to the river and the road some time. There's no real danger in a mist, so long as you keep your head. Snow's the thing to be afraid of. Never come up on the hill if you think it's going to snow. Once it's down, it's all right, so long as you're dressed for it, but never be out when it's falling. Promise?' She nodded again. She felt docile and at ease. She had completely lost control of the situation, but she did not mind.

He let go of her arms, and they stood there, a little apart, with the black rock towering over them and the white mist swirling round them. He looked grave and concerned, but almost detached, as if he was dealing with a child. There was nothing of the gay seducer about him at all. The enormous physical attraction she had felt no longer melted her, but suddenly and for the first time she liked him enormously. The liking was no more reasonable than the attraction, but just as compelling. 'I'm sorry,' she said. 'I wasn't really scared, but it was a bit disconcerting, coming down suddenly like that. I thought it was just going to rain.'

He shook his head. 'It won't rain,' he said. 'We're in the cloud, not under it. We'll get out of it a bit farther down. I'll see you down the path that far. Then you can find your own way.'

This was the cue for her to assert her independence, but she did not feel independent in the least. She said, 'Oh well, thank you, if you could.' It was all very civilised and considerate and totally unromantic.

He said, 'I think we'd better start straight away, if you don't mind. It's bound to be rather slow going, and you don't want to be late.'

She did not, indeed, want to be late. That was the one thing she did not want, but she found she did not resent his knowing this. 'I'm ready,' she said. 'Shall I go ahead?'

'No, better let me, if you don't mind. I know the path. I'll take it easy. Just follow me as closely as you can.'

He went past her and started off down the path, and she turned and went after him. Their small world went with them, just the few yards of twisting uneven path shut in by the white infinity of mist. Neither of them said anything. Close beside them, but out of sight, the burn kept up its unending monologue, but nothing else broke the silence. Sometimes she lifted her eyes to take in the broad, easily moving figure ahead of her, but mainly she watched his feet, stepping carefully where he stepped. Her only worry now was that she might miss her footing. She was no longer worried about time.

She did not know how long they had been walking when she saw darkness ahead. The cloud still hung there, but from beyond it the shadowed colourless world was starting to show through. A moment later he stopped and turned. She walked on to where he was standing, and this time he gathered her in his arms and kissed her. It was a hard, fierce kiss, and her head fell back and she opened her lips to his, because she did not know where she was with him at all, and her defences were quite down.

When he took his mouth from hers, she pushed herself away from him and said, 'I didn't come here for this.'

'I know that. Never mind. There's no harm done.'

She said, 'But there is, there is.' She almost wailed at him. He stood there, his arms hanging loose at his sides, looking at her. His face was as hard and uncompromising as his kiss had been. She said, 'James —' but he shook his head.

'Not now,' he said. 'You haven't got time and you won't get it right. You go on down. You won't get lost now. I'll go back up the corrie.'

She said, 'You will be all right?'

He smiled at her, and they were back suddenly to their earlier friendliness. He said, 'Of course I'll be all right. What do you take me for? Go on now, or you really will be late.'

She was utterly at a loss, but there was nothing she could do. 'All right,' she said. 'Goodbye, James.'

He said, 'Goodbye, Catriona,' and stood aside, and she went past him down the path. Almost at once the mist fell away in front of her, and she saw the bottom of the glen, as she had seen it once before, like a tunnel of darkness under its roof of hanging cloud. The road and river would be straight ahead under the curve of the hill. To her left there would be the school buildings and the bridge. She would see them when she came round the eastern shoulder. She went a little way down the path and then stopped and looked back.

The bottom of the cloud lay across the corrie like a wall above her. It could not really be as solid as it looked, only she did not know how far she could see into it. She hoped she might still see him standing there, but at first she saw nothing. Then, back in the uncertain edge of the cloud, a figure moved. It moved sideways for a moment and then vanished again. It did not look as if it was on the path, but she could not be certain. She did not think it moved as James moved, but she could not be certain of that either. It was just a figure moving not quite where she expected to see one. It did not do anything. She turned and went down into the leaden daylight. She could see the path clearly now, and after a bit she started to run. She knew this was not sensible, but she could not help herself. She ran until she was over the brow of the slope and out of sight of anyone who might be watching her from under the edge of the cloud. Then she began walking again. Her run had been all downhill. She was not too badly out of breath, but she had a stitch in her side, and her legs had no strength in them. She collected herself before she came to the bridge, and she walked up the school drive with a steady unconcerned stride, as if she had been out for a walk and was back in time for lunch, as indeed she was. She took the main path past the front of the Haskells' house. She looked at the windows as she passed, but could see no one there. She had just turned up the path to her house when Richard called 'Kate!' from behind her.

She stopped and turned. He was quite close to her already. She said, 'Oh, Richard.'

He looked at her with a sort of sharp concern. He said, 'What's the matter?'

She shook her head. 'Nothing. It's all right. I got caught in the mist, that's all. It came down very suddenly, and I couldn't see a thing. It upset me a bit, but I'm all right now. Sorry. It was silly of me.'

She turned and went on ahead of him. She had a sudden panic that her lipstick might be smeared. It was a nasty, rather shameful apprehension, the vulgar detail of intrigue which she was not used to and had not thought of. But she could do nothing about it now. She walked on in the grey light with her back to him, hoping it was all right.

The house was dark when they got inside it, but she did not put on a light. She stopped in the hall to take her waterproofs off. Richard had no coat on, and went straight through into the kitchen. When she had got her things off, she switched on the light and looked at herself quickly in the glss in the hall. Her mouth was perfectly all right, but she did not like the look on her face.

When she went into the kitchen, he said, 'Sorry you had a fright I don't know – I suppose it's all right your going out on the hill like this? It's a wild sort of place.'

She was suddenly angry, with a mixture of relief and apprehension. She said, 'Of course it's all right. Where else is there to go? Besides, I like it.'

He was all reason at once. 'That's perfectly true,' he said. 'I didn't mean to fuss. So long as you're none the worse.'

'I told you,' she said, 'I'm all right now.' She did not feel all right at all. She did not think she even looked it. 'I'm a bit cold,' she said. 'Could we have something hot?'

He said, 'Soup? I'll open a tin. It's the quickest thing.'

'Oh yes, please. I'll go and change my stockings. They're damp. The rest of me's all right.' She went through into the bedroom, leaving him busy in the kitchen. She switched on the light and went and looked at herself hard in the glass. The eyes stared back at her and the mouth was drawn down at the corners. Portrait of a guilty wife, she thought. In a part of her mind she knew it was nonsense. All the same, the thing could not go on. Then she sat down on the bed and peeled off her damp stockings.

Merely to be dry was a comfort, and the soup put fresh heart into her. The kitchen was warm and the whole house pleasant to be in. They talked with amicable detachment about things at the school. Presently he would go back to the school, and then the house would be hers, and she could sit with only the reading lamp on beside her chair and perhaps get herself sorted out a bit.

IX

She had been walking for some time when she saw the figure on the skyline. It was quite motionless. It stood there, slightly hunched, and she knew it was looking down at her on the road. The cloud had lifted clear of the hill by the time she came out, but she had no intention of walking anywhere but on the tarmac. The sky was still dark and threatening, and the figure stood there, lighter than the towering hill under it, but just darker than the sky. It leant on something, a stick or a gun, she could not see which. She stopped and looked up at it, but it still did not move. It was not James. It was Alec, of course. It must be. She remembered him as she had first seen him on the station platform, waiting with motionless concentration for his master to emerge from the train. He had reminded her of an animal then. Very few people ever stood as still as that. A hunting animal, waiting. That was what he was, after all, bred to it. But she did not like his watching her.

She wanted badly to do something to break his concentration, even to establish some sort of human communication with him. But there was nothing she could do except wave, and that was absurd. She turned and walked on, conscious all the time of the scrutiny from above. It was a condition of life here, and she must get used to it. Mentally or physically, there was always somebody on the watch She walked on steadily, determined not to look up again, but after a bit the thing was too much for her. She did not stop this time, but she turned her head and looked up at the hill as she walked. There was a second figure beside him now, and her heart jumped. But even this was not James. It was a slighter figure altogether, and as she looked up, it raised an arm and waved to her. She stopped and waved back. There was nothing else she could do. As she stood there, looking up at them, both figures moved.

Alec turned and went back, and a moment later had disappeared over the skyline. The other man began coming down the hill-face, straight towards her. He moved with what seemed astonishing speed and agility, almost running, occasionally even jumping, taking everything in his stride in his undeviating line down the hill. He was a slight, wiry figure, his legs encased in something dark and close-fitting, not the baggy knickerbocker breeches which James and Alec wore on the hill. He was half-way down before she recognised him. It was Mr Godwin. The gymnast, of course. It would take a gymnast to come down the hill like that. What he was doing up on the hill with Alec she could not imagine, but because of this very incongruity she was glad to see him. She stood and waited for him to come.

The slope was easier now, and he was definitely running. His eyes were fixed on the ground in front of him, but he knew she was watching him. Every movement was calculated. He was like a ballet dancer, concentrating on the perfection of his own movement, but conscious all the time of his audience. It was only when he was not more than fifteen yards from her that he lifted his face and gave her his sharp, impish grin. A moment later he was beside her on the road, breathing fast but easily and well able to talk.

'Hullo,' he said. 'Out walking?'

'Yes,' she said. 'But I think I've come far enough.'

He nodded. 'May I walk back with you, then?'

'Of course.' She turned, and he fell into step beside her. His stride was no longer than hers. She felt more cheerful at once. She felt safe with Mr Godwin. She had heard that women did feel safe with men like that. He was not the first one she had met, obviously. It was only that up to now she had felt safe, if safe was the word, with everyone. Now that there was someone capable of turning her mental peace upside down with the lift of an eyebrow, she felt an immediate and almost cosy pleasure in the company of a man who could not, and did not want to. She said, 'What in the world were you doing up on the hill with yon Alec?'

He turned and flashed a quick inquisitive glance at her. 'You know him?' he said.

'I've seen him. I can't say I reckon him among my closest friends. To be honest, he gives me the creeps. Doesn't he you?'

He shook his head. All his gestures and expressions were quick and very slightly extravagant. 'I know what you mean,' he said. 'Definitely *louche*. He even smells like an animal. Not like an unwashed man, but like an animal. Not unpleasant. Had you noticed? No, you wouldn't. But enormously interesting. In more ways than one.'

He walked on, smiling his little smile. He was full of a tremendous vitality. He wanted her to ask him, and she did. 'Interesting how?' she said.

'Well. Interesting in himself. Anthropologically, if you like. A surviving specimen of primitive man, meshed uneasily into civilisation and enslaved by alcohol. Caliban, you know? But with a whole range of capacities we haven't got. When the bombs fall on our civilisation, it will be the Alecs who survive and breed. People all the isle with Calibans.'

Kate nodded, smiling. She did not believe a word of it, but she enjoyed hearing him talk. 'How else?' she said.

'Ah. On a naughtier and more mundane level. He observes the world of men from behind the bars of his cage. He has been observing it for – what? – sixty years, I suppose, and he hasn't missed a thing. He knows it all. You could dignify it by saying he is a repository of oral tradition, in the best anthropological manner. He may be that,

81

too, for all I know. He probably knows who slew the Red Fox of Appin, if anyone cares, which I for one do not. More to the point, he is the perfect treasure-house of local gossip.'

'The whisper in the glen in person?'

She said it lightly enough, but he considered it seriously. She could see him considering it seriously, because he meant her to see it. He was considering the thing seriously, and this was what considering a thing seriously looked like. He was a one-man melodrama, and very good company.

'Not really,' he said, 'no.'

'But you said he knew all the local gossip.'

'He knows it, yes. But he doesn't pass it on. Or very little. He is the original primeval silence. You must have noticed.'

'Then how do you know he knows it all?'

'Because of the way he talks when he does talk. It is implicit, but it is there, in the back of his mind. All you see is one small facet at a time, but if you see enough facets, you can guess at the underlying shape. Or of course you can try making him drunk, but that is a job for heroes or millionaires.'

She laughed and shook her head. 'I still don't know what you were doing up on the hill with him. Shouldn't you be working?'

'Ah, that. I was working, in fact. I'm in charge of the adventure projects. We do them on Macalister's domains. I was out plotting the new course, and Alec was told off to accompany me. I'm not quite sure why. Perhaps to see I didn't shoot a stag with my catapult and bring it home on my shoulders. All the same, he's worth a guinea a minute on the hill. It's like being personally conducted by an elderly dog-fox. You have to ask him questions the whole time, because he assumes that you see what he sees, which of course you don't, but I'm quite shameless about asking questions. As I am, indeed, about most things.'

She was not going to be diverted by a lead like that. She said, 'What in the world are the adventure projects?'

'Oh – sorry. I'm as bad as yon Alec. Assuming you know things when there's no reason why you should. I thought perhaps your husband might have mentioned them.'

'Not by name. Still, I can guess the kind of thing. Initiative and survival and all that. Finding your way across country with a compass and sleeping in a cave with pemmican for breakfast. That sort of thing.'

He brought one hand down with a hard slap on one of his lean, muscular thighs, and doubled up with laughter. 'Pemmican!' he said. 'I hadn't thought of that. Where can I get it, do you suppose? Fortnum's?'

'You could try. Why can't they let the poor little devils do it in the summer?'

'Tst, tst. Kid's stuff. In any case, they'd be eaten alive by midges until they got well up on the ben. We don't let them go if it's snowing, of course, or we really might lose some of them. But the idea is to make them as wet and cold as possible without actually killing them. Makes men of them, by God, or something.'

'And you're in charge of all this?'

'That's right. Don't sound so surprised. I'm very good on the hill, in fact. I could survive as well as most, for all my pretty ways.'

'Along with the Calibans? Only you wouldn't be peopling the isle, is that it?'

He gave her a bright, hard smile. 'Not personally, I think. How did you guess?'

She shook her head. She said, 'That's a very expensive looking camera you've got.' She had only just noticed it. He wore it slung from his shoulder, but in the small of his back, where it was safe, not on his navel like an American tourist.

'Not only looks,' he said. 'It is, damnably expensive. That's another of the things I'm good at. I'll show you some time, if you like. Deer and things. I'm waiting until I get enough real sizzlers to make a book, and then I'm going to go south and hit the wild-life market. There's money in it, only you've got to invest heavily or it's no good. Hence this almost supernatural machine.' He turned and surveyed her steadily as he walked beside her. Surveyed was the word. It was a long appraising stare, but there was no offence in it. He said, 'I'd like to photograph you some time, if you'd let me. That bone's marvellous. Pure upper-class Highland. Was your father anything special – clan-wise, I mean?'

'I don't think so. I mean – not *the* Macinnes or anything. I don't think there is one, in fact. If there was, I'd have heard, all right.'

'Well, anyway, the genes came through beautifully. You've only got to compare our Janet. Highland, presum-ably, but a different stock altogether. And she knows it. Hence part at least of the resentment.'

It occurred to Kate that she should not be discussing the headmaster's wife in these terms with a junior member of the staff, but she did not yet feel like a schoolmaster's wife, and propriety was no match for curiosity. In any case, Mr Godwin was quite irrepressible. He would say what he wanted to say unless she got angry with him, and she did not want to do that. She said, 'I don't know how you know that. All I know is that she seemed terribly put out when I told I was as Highland as she was. Which I'm not, presumably, but she provoked me into saying it.'

He nodded and smiled. 'She would be,' he said. 'I wish I'd been there. The class difference was always obvious, you see, but so long as you were English, it didn't matter. Different league. But once you were in the same league, the difference can't be ignored. No wonder she was upset.'

Kate said, 'I thought she was just upset because she didn't know. A failure of the intelligence system.'

He looked at her again. He was full of admiration, but with him it didn't matter. 'My goodness,' he said, 'you're learning fast. Anyway, I haven't tried to photograph Janet. Make a marvellous nude, though, wouldn't she? *Playboy* would pay a lot for her.' He mused, visibly, on wasted opportunity. He said, 'Perhaps they've got a bathroom window or something.'

She said, 'You'll be losing your job if you don't look out,' and he sighed.

'You're quite right,' he said. 'The game is too heavily preserved. But it was a nice thought.' Then he cheered up. 'Anyway,' he said, 'it's your head I want. With a hill background. Make a marvellous picture. Would your husband mind, do you think?'

'You'd better ask him. But for my sake, don't let Janet hear you, if that's how she feels. I've got to live in this place.'

'I won't, I promise you.'

When they were in sight of the bridge, he said, 'I'll go on, I think, if you don't mind.'

She said, 'Playing safe?' and he gave her another of his quick flashes of admiration.

'If you like. But your safety as much as mine. More, in fact. You're more vulnerable.'

He said it in a perfectly matter-of-fact sort of way, but it struck suddenly cold on her new-found cheerfulness. 'All right,' she said. 'Off you go.'

They both stopped and looked at each other. He said, 'By God, you're nice.' He raised a hand in a wonderfully comprehensive gesture of blessing and farewell. Then he turned and started to run. She stood and watched him go, partly because she wanted to let him get well ahead and partly for the sheer pleasure of seeing him run. When he had turned over the bridge, she started to walk on again. She thought about Mr Godwin with an uncomfortable mixture of solace and apprehension. He had offered her his friendship, perhaps rather an alliance, at least a benevolent neutrality. She was glad of this, but at the same time she was now a little afraid of him. After their first meeting she had sensed danger in him, and Richard had agreed that it might be there. He had not gone out of his way to warn her against Mr Godwin, as he had against Janet Haskell – and how right he had been there – but he had done nothing to allay the apprehension she felt. Now Mr Godwin had tried to allay it himself. To a large extent he had succeeded, but not altogether. There was a bottomless quality in him which the mind could find no rest on. Shameless in everything, he had said. The words were a characteristic exaggeration, but she thought she knew what he meant. He was as neutral as the sky, and no more subject to the rules. All the same, he was good company, and she needed company very badly. On balance she was glad of him.

Later, when they had had their tea, she said, 'I walked part of the way home with Mr Godwin. He had been out on the hill plotting these extraordinary exercises or whatever it is they do. He was very amusing about it.'

Richard said, 'Oh? Yes, that's right. They haven't tried to involve me, thank goodness. He doesn't fit the picture somehow, does he?'

She laughed. 'I'm afraid I said more or less the same. He quite took me up on it. He said he was very good on the hill for all his pretty ways. He is, too. I saw him come down the face when I was walking on the road. An astonishing performance. He's an odd person, all right, but I think I rather like him. At least he's amusing. He wants to photograph me.'

He raised his eyebrows and nodded. 'Does he?' he said. 'That's quite a compliment, coming from him. I mean, an aesthetic judgement with no strings to it. And he takes his photography very seriously. I've only seen one or two of his things at the school, but they're very good. I think you should feel flattered.'

'Flattered enough to let him do it?'

'Oh, I don't see why not, so long as he promises not to pin you up anywhere. I'd like to see what he makes of you. Did he say anything else of interest? He'd talk to you as he wouldn't to most of us, and I shouldn't think he misses much.'

For a moment she hesitated. Then she said, 'He more or less warned me against Mrs Haskell.'

'Did he? Well, so did I, if it comes to that. What did he say?'

She said, 'As a matter of fact, it was very interesting. And I should think very shrewd. As you say, I don't think he misses much. He said she resented my social superiority particularly because I was a Highlander. If I had been mere English, it wouldn't have mattered. A different league was how he put it.'

He raised his eyebrows again. 'Mm,' he said. 'Yes, that's very well observed.She does take refuge in her Scottishness. I expect she does it with Haskell, too. But if you're on the inside already, she has no defences. And you see, there's really no one else in her immediate circle – the school, I mean. Most of the staff are bachelors. There are one or two wives, but nothing very exciting, I don't think. There's the secretary and the domestic bursar, but they're wage-slaves, after all. So she was queen of Glenaidon until you came along. Of course you're liable to put her nose out of joint. And she hasn't got the mere social know-how to carry it off. Well, you've been warned. Twice now, in fact. I don't think she could make trouble with Haskell – I mean, trouble for us – but she might make trouble for him, and I wouldn't want that, either. The great thing is to give her nothing she

87

can get hold of.'

Kate said, 'They don't need anything up here. They make it. It's no longer dirks and Lochaber axes, it's just their tongues, but the stabbing and hacking still goes on. It's only that you don't see the blood.'

'That's not your Highland blood stirring,' he said. 'That's your old anti-bodies arming themselves against it.' He got up from his chair and stood for a moment looking down at her. 'Let the galled jade wince,' he said. 'Our withers are unwrung.' Then he went out and left her sitting there. When he came back, he had his books and papers with him, and they sat so, in silence, until she went out to get the supper.

X

She was walking out of the Aberwhinnie car park when Mrs Grant hailed her from across the street, and she stopped and went over to her. 'How nice to see you,' Mrs Grant said. 'I've been meaning to get in touch with you. Are you furiously busy? If not, come and have a cup of coffee. I'm longing for one, and it's a bit cold-blooded doing it on one's own. Like secret drinking.'

'I'd love to,' said Kate. 'No, I'm in no particular hurry. Just ordinary shopping. Where can one get it?'

'There's only one place. It's called the Eightsome Reel, I'm afraid, and it's a tripper-trap in season, but they're quite glad to see one at this time of the year, and the coffee's all right.'

'That sounds fine. I've been wondering if there was anywhere, but it didn't look hopeful.'

'I know. Come on. I'll show you.'

Even out of season the Eightsome Reel had a window full of deerskin purses and tartan scarves and astonishingly ugly brooches set with polished lumps of the local stones. Inside there were small tables with hand woven cloths and heavy art pottery. Farther south the women might have worn smocks, but here they had tartan skirts and fluffy jumpers. They greeted Mrs Grant by name and looked at Kate with bright, predatory curiosity. But the coffee, as Mrs Grant had promised, was good. 'I've had you on my conscience a bit,' she said, 'ever since we met at James's. I've been meaning to ask you and Richard over. I was afraid you might be rather bored out there at the end of the glen.'

'No,' said Kate. 'Not really. I'm still getting a kick out

of the place. And I suppose coming to grips with my ancestral prejudices. Even Richard said I ought to wear the tartan.'

'Well, there you are. I told you you'd have to compromise. It's rather a nice one, yours, all blues and greens. Ours is a bit startling, to tell the truth, only don't tell Malcolm I said so. Bain's will do you a quite respectable skirt, if you don't want to go fifty miles for it, and you'd wear it like a charm. You think about it.'

'I will, I promise. Perhaps the next time I come in. Only don't rush me. I had too much of it as a child, and I'm still getting over it.'

'You will, I'm sure. It was nice the other evening, wasn't it? James is a very good host, and he makes himself very comfortable. Nothing like the state the old man kept, but still very comfortable. In fact, he's too comfortable by half. And too attractive. It's time he settled down and got married and provided himself with an heir. Otherwise there's only a cousin over in Edinburgh, and goodness knows what he'd make of it. You need to be bred to a place like that.'

'Yes,' said Kate, 'I suppose so.' Her mind was back on its different levels again. On the upper level it discoursed pleasantly with Mrs Grant on the desirability of finding James a suitable wife. Underneath the mere idea filled her with an almost terrifying dismay. She said, 'I wondered why he hadn't married before.'

'I don't think he felt up to it while the old man was still alive. There wasn't much they didn't disagree about, and a wife would have been a fresh cause of upset. And of course, she'd have found it pretty tough going, whoever she was. And I fancy there wasn't much money to spare, anyway. But now he's free to please himself, and after all, he's got himself some ready money, even if he had to set the glen by the ears doing it. So I think it's time he got on with it. I'll tell him so one of these days. Otherwise he'll be getting himself into trouble again, and this time he won't have the old man there to read the Riot Act.'

The two halves of Kate's mind came together with an almost audible click. This was a thing she had to know about. There was something Mrs Haskell had said, a Mrs Somebody, whose husband had been at the school. She could not remember the name. She found Mrs Grant looking at her. She sipped her coffee and summoned up a smile. 'I did hear something,' she said. 'Somebody at the school, wasn't it?'

'She wasn't at the school then,' said Mrs Grant. 'Janet Cameron, she was then. Her mother was a widow-woman along the glen.'

For what seemed a very long time Kate's mind stopped working altogether. The meaning of what Mrs Grant had said came straight into it, and her mind simply threw it out. After that it did nothing. All this time Mrs Grant was looking at her, and she allowed herself, because this was in order, to show on her face some trace of the confusion she felt. Mrs Grant said, 'I've startled you, I can see.' She seemed pleased, but there was no malice in it.

Kate said, 'You don't mean —'

'Janet Haskell, as now is. Her mother lived along the glen, and Janet was a secretary or something. I can't say I can see the attraction myself, but of course she was a fine big bundle of woman, and you know what men are. She still is, for that matter. To do James justice, I feel sure his intentions were strictly dishonourable, but you can imagine what hers would have been, and he might have found himself in a jam. The thing doesn't bear thinking about, really. Anyway, I expect it got talked about, and from all accounts the old man came down on James like a ton of bricks. There was a final God Almighty row, apparently, and James went south and stayed there. He may even have gone abroad for a bit. And then the next thing we heard, she'd caught the poor little schoolmaster. Next best thing, I suppose. Then at very much the same time the old man was killed and James had to come home. From what I've heard, he's played it very careful ever since. But as I say, he's an attractive person, and he hasn't got enough to occupy him. No one has up here. The lairds are just as bad as the rest. So I reckon it's high time he found himself something suitable and settled down, before he makes a fool of himself with something young enough to be his daughter. That'll be the next thing, if he doesn't watch out. He'll be that sort of age soon.' She smiled cheerfully at Kate over her coffee. 'Can't you find him someone?' she said. 'Haven't you got a sister or something? There's next to nothing suitable round these parts, and he won't lift a finger for himself.'

Kate shook her head and smiled cheerfully back. The immediate danger of being actually sick had passed, but she wondered what colour her face was. At least it was not red. She felt cold, cold down to the pit of her stomach, and her palms were clammy. She continued to smile. 'You do surprise me,' she said. 'Do you know Mrs Haskell?'

'Well – I've met her, of course. But only at school do's and so on. You know the kind of thing. One is supposed to go, being the local school, but I can't say I care for it myself. You can't see Malcolm sending the boys there, can you? They went to Glenalmond, of course, but they've finished with it now, thank goodness. What does Richard think of it, now he's seen a bit more of it?'

Back to the school, thought Kate. The school was already getting to be her conversational staple. She could talk brightly about it, even to Richard, while her mind was occupied with something completely different. Now her mind presented her with a remorselessly clear picture of James taking the massive and presumably virginal Janet in his arms. His hands strayed over those bulging softnesses as they had not strayed over her. The more the flesh, the more the attraction, presumably. You know what men are. But what would he find to say to a woman like that? What was there in all that body to talk to? But it would not be conversation he was after, damn him, damn him, damn all men. She said, 'I think he's quite enjoying the work side of it. He says there are some quite bright boys in his lot, however they got there, and of course he's trying to boost them up into something worth teaching.'

'Oh good,' said Mrs Grant. 'I can't see him sticking it out indefinitely in a complete intellectual wilderness. He's too good for that, isn't he?'

Too good. Of course, that was what he was. She knew him and his vanities and oddities through and through, and she kept a lot of herself, more and more nowadays, out of his reach altogether, but for all that, there he was, too good for her, bound by rules which he had probably never spelt out to himself, but which she had thrown overboard at the first lift of James Macalister's eyebrow. She smiled the coy smile of the good little wife accepting a compliment to her husband as a compliment to herself and deprecating it gracefully. She said, 'Well, he does take his subject seriously, of course. He has never given up his reading, you know, not even when we were in Africa. I mean, the journals and so on. Books weren't easy, of course. He's even published a bit. Only short things, I mean, not books.'

Mrs Grant said, 'Mr Haskell's very lucky to get him. He's a clever man himself, I think. Malcolm says so, anyhow. Which makes it all the worse his marrying that woman. She can't have a brain in her head. But then I don't suppose it was her head he married her for.' She drank the last of her coffee and peered into the bottom of her cup regretfully. 'I must be getting on,' she said, 'and I expect you must, too. Shall we go?' When they were outside, she said, 'Bain's is just down there on the left. Go and have a look at it, anyway. It's not at all bad. I don't know if they'll have the Macinnes, but if they haven't, they'll get it for you.'

'Yes,' said Kate. 'Yes, I will. Thank you.'

'Goodbye, then. I'll give you a ring, may I, and fix a date for you to come and see us?'

'Yes,' said Kate again, 'thank you, that would be nice.' They went their different ways along the narrow streets between the prosperous local shops, and she pulled her mind back to what she had to do. It was not until she had finished her shopping and was back on the twisting road that she let her mind go again. She did not like the way it went, but it would not go anywhere else. She was still shaken by the violence of her feelings. She had taken the unknown Mrs What's-her-name at the school in her stride. She was a shadowy figure at best, and there had been an instinctive refusal to let anything Mrs Haskell said affect her in any way. Now she was suddenly faced with Janet Haskell herself, Janet very much in the flesh, all that pink flesh and ginger hair, and yet James found her desirable, whether his intentions had been dishonourable or not. She wanted to drive straight home and charge him with it, in the desperate hope that he could clear himself, like Regan and the smooth-spoken Edmund.

> *I am doubtful that you have been conjunct*
> *And bosomed with her, as far as we call hers.*

As far as we call hers, to the forfended place. That was another jealous woman letting her imagination rip to her own incredulous disgust, and with no more moral justification than she herself had. Conjunct and bosomed with her, and all that bosom to be conjunct with. God, she thought, an ounce of civet, good apothecary, to sweeten my imagination.

Then she thought, but she wouldn't have let him. She would have been too careful for that. There was cold blood in that big body and a calculating mind. She would have kept him out until he had paid the full price of admission, and he had not paid. She took a sort of comfort from her adversary's probable scruples, knowing all the time that she would have had none herself, and was at once appalled by the degradation which such comfort brought with it. The road cut sharply round the shoulder of a hill, and in her fury she nearly put a wheel over the edge. The physical scare brought her to her senses, and she pulled the car back on to the centre of the narrow road and cut it down to a more reasonable speed. When she came to the end of the loch, she took the south road, so that there would be no chance of seeing James or his possessions, and drove with a sort of controlled desperation past the bungalow where the quiet, sharp couple lived and the camp and the little stone house where Mrs Somebody had lived until the camp had driven her out of it.

She had lived at such speed ever since she had parted with Mrs Grant that she got home long before lunch-time. Richard had not come up from the school, and she did not know whether he would. He did not always come back at this time, and it was agreed that he should please himself in the matter and need not let her know. They did not go in for set lunches. She went straight into the kitchen and unpacked and put away her shopping. She did not know what she could do until lunch-time, and wondered whether it would be better or worse if she had a drink. Then the telephone rang in the hall.

This time she had no doubt at all who it would be or, when she heard his voice, who it was. He said, 'Catriona? Look, I'm sorry about the other morning, but it was Act of God, after all. I think we should have our talk, all the same. I was wondering – could you come up the corrie tomorrow, do you think? I wish you would.'

If he had sounded calm and businesslike, as he had before, she might have refused, but he did not. He sounded urgent and diffident, and her anger melted helplessly even before she found her voice to speak to him. She said, 'Oh, James. Yes. Yes, all right. Same time and place?'

'Yes,' he said. 'What's the matter? You sound upset.'

'Do I? Sorry. No, nothing's the matter. All right, tomorrow, then.'

He said, 'Yes, please.'

She said, 'All right, James,' and put the receiver down. She turned, as she had after Janet Haskell's visit, and leant back against the inside of the front door, head back, gazing through the open doors into the sitting-room and kitchen and at the shut door of the bedroom she shared with Richard. Only now she had shut no enemy out. The enemy was within, inside her home, inside herself, an enemy she had fostered and now could not get rid of. Not yet. That was what it always came back to. The thing could not simply be left as it was. How it should be before it could be left she did not let herself think.

She heard Richard come up to the door only a moment before he put his hand on the handle. She spun away from it as if it had burnt her, and was facing him in the hall when he opened the door. If she had been talking to James when he came in, she could not have felt more guiltily startled. And yet all she had been doing was thinking. It was an odd place to think, but that did not in itself call for explanations. They stared at each other blankly and recovered at the same moment. He said, 'Good Lord, you startled me.'

'I didn't hear you coming,' she said. 'I was just going out. I didn't know if you'd be back.' She wondered why all the most direct lies seemed to be the innocent and unnecessary ones.

96

He stood back from the door, but she shook her head. 'I wasn't going anywhere,' she said. 'Just to stretch my legs before lunch. I've been shopping. But now you've come, let's have lunch.'

He said, 'I'm in no hurry, if you'd like a walk first,' but she was exasperated now by his deference to a need she had only invented.

'No, no,' she said, 'I don't want to go out now,' and he nodded and came in.

He said, 'Godwin asked my permission to take some photos of you. He was most formal about it, and curiously confidential. Rather as if he was asking permission to pay his addresses to a marriageable daughter. Which is the last thing I can imagine him asking anybody.'

She laughed. Even the mention of Mr Godwin made her feel safe again. 'Well, you know,' she said, 'he's perfectly right. Not only to ask you, I mean. As a matter of fact I told him to, though I didn't imagine he'd take it so seriously. But I mean the confidentiality. It seems to me one can't be too careful in a place like this. People can make something of anything.'

He said, 'Not with Godwin, surely. But maybe you're right. Anyway, I solemnly assured him that I had been consulted, and had no objection. Does that satisfy you?'

'Of course,' she said. 'Did he say when?'

'This afternoon, he said. He's got the afternoon free, and the light's right, apparently. So you'd better make your preparations.'

She laughed again. 'Not on your life,' she said. 'He can take me as he finds me. Let's have lunch first, anyway. I don't want to come out looking hungry.'

They were eating when the phone rang again, and she got up at once 'Shall I go?' he said, but she was already half-way to the door. The voice said, 'Mrs Wychett? Or may I call you Kate? It's Peter Godwin speaking.' His voice over the phone had a curious vibrant quality. It went with her picture of him, but she had not noticed it when she was with him.

'Oh, hullo,' she said. 'I gather you want to take your pictures this afternoon?'

'Please,' he said, 'if you don't mind.'

'I don't mind at all.'

'Oh good. Well, look. I'm going out now to find the best place. If you come out when you're ready, I'll meet you somewhere about where we met the other day. Will that be all right?'

'Yes. Yes, all right. I'll start in about half an hour.'

'Good. See you then. Goodbye for now.'

'Goodbye,' said Kate, and put the receiver down. She went back to Richard in the kitchen. 'Mr Godwin,' she said. 'As discreet as ever. I'm going alone in half an hour's time.'

He nodded. 'It all seems unduly tortuous,' he said.

'That's the place,' she said. 'I still think he's right.'

He shook his head but said nothing.

XI

Mr Godwin said, 'I hope you don't mind my making you climb all this way. I badly want a distant background.'

'I don't mind,' said Kate. 'I'm sorry if I'm holding you up. I can't go your pace.'

'That's practice. We're nearly there.'

As they came over the brow of the hill, he pointed to a small rock. 'I thought there,' he said. Ahead of them, northwards, the mountains hung layer behind overlapping layer, green-brown fading to grey and grey to blue, and the blue rising at last to white under the pale, clear sky. He said, 'It'll be all snow presently. It's not so interesting then. But given a bit of sun, this first snow on the high tops is always terrific. If you sit there and I come at you from a pretty low angle, there'll be nothing between you and the Grampians, which is what I want.'

Kate sat. The sun was warm on her skin and the wind ruffled her hair. She felt happy and at peace. There was no embarrassment in the thing at all, because Peter Godwin was not like that. She was ready to pour her warmth and happiness into the camera, so that James could have it to keep. That he would have the photographs when they were done she took for granted. That was what they were for. The practical difficulties she did not examine.

'Kate.' All this time he had been fiddling with his camera at a little distance from her, and now she turned and smiled at him. She heard him draw in his breath in a sharp hiss, and there was a subdued click from the camera. He lowered the camera from in front of his face, and for a moment they stared at each other. He looked more moved than she had ever seen him look, or thought he could. 'Oh my dear,' he said, 'I only hope somebody's worth it,' and she did not ask him what he meant. He lowered his eyes and was fiddling with the camera again. 'Come on,' he said. 'We'll try a few more. But unless something goes wrong, that was it. No, don't watch the dicky-bird this time. Look at the landscape. Look at anything you like. Me, if you like. Don't try to keep still or anything. I'll take a chance on what I can see of you. And of course talk if you want to.'

She looked obediently away from him and asked what she wanted to know. She said, 'How long have the Haskells been married?'

He spoke, then and for some time afterwards, in a curiously subdued, preoccupied tone, as if most of his mind was on his subject and his camera. He said, 'Oh – three or four years, I suppose. She came as secretary. Did you know? The real woman got ill and was given three months' leave, so Janet, from along the glen, was drafted in. She didn't need the three months, anything like. She made up her mind the first week and settled the thing in six weeks or so. It was sad to see, but what to do? You can't tell your headmaster he's being a fool.'

She turned and looked at him, and as her face came round, she heard the camera click again. After that it clicked at intervals as they talked, until she no longer thought about it. It was an easy way of being photographed.

'And what now?' she said. 'Does it work? I can't make out.'

'Well – she's no use to him in his job, of course. But people know her here. She's part of the landscape and can be taken for granted. If he moved, she could be disastrous.'

'Yes. Yes, that was what Richard said when he first met her. But I mean – how does he see it?'

He did not answer for some time. It was as if he had only half his mind to spare, and for this particular question this was not enough. Presently he said. 'He's one of the quiet ones, you know, Haskell. It's never easy to tell what he's really thinking. He seems to know exactly what he wants to say. And he's got wit, too, and charm in a subdued sort of way. It's not easy to see under all that to what makes him tick. But I mean – he could have only one reason for marrying her, surely. And that's still there, presumably. Unless he's fed up with it by now. So I suppose it's all right.'

She could not look at him now, but she had to ask the question. 'What about her?' she said.

'I don't know,' he said. 'You know more about these things than I do. It seems to me that Haskell is a little man for all that woman. He wasn't even the one she wanted, anyway.'

'No?' She suddenly found her mouth set hard, and tried to soften it. Mr Godwin said nothing for a bit, and when he spoke, his voice seemed hesitant.

'Well – one only knows what one's told. There was some talk of her setting her cap at the laird. Then he went south – the old man ws still alive then, of course – and she settled for Haskell. I must say, from what I've seen of him, I'd say he had more sense – and better taste, if it comes to that. If she laid herself out for it, he may have had a flutter with her. She'd be all right for that, I suppose, if you like coarse fishing. But he'd never have married her in a hundred years. He's no foolish virgin, the laird, not like poor old Haskell. Not by a long chalk. Anyway, then there was this business of her mother, and now, as you know, she can't find names bad enough for him.'

Kate's head came round with a jerk, but this time he lowered the camera and sighed. 'What about her mother?' she said.

'Oh well, she lived in a house where the holiday camp is now. That was the Cameron family home. The mother was a widow. So long as the old laird was there, she was all right, but when James sold, she had to get out. I'm not sure whose house it was, but that doesn't matter much. She'd have had to go anyway. By that time Janet was Mrs Haskell, just about, so she wasn't personally involved. But of course she took it hard. So you see, it isn't only the honour of the glen that makes her go on so about the camp. Anyway, that's her ostensible reason for being so anti-laird. For myself, I should say there's more to it than that, but that'll do for public consumption.' He looked down at his camera, sighed again and started shutting it down. 'Let's call it a day,' he said. 'I can't photograph you when you look like that.'

Kate got up from her rock and turned her face to the distant mountains. She shivered suddenly. She felt chilled all through, as if the huge cold of the hill had seeped into her unawares as she sat. The sun still shone, but all the peace and contentment had gone out of her. 'All right,' she said. 'Let's go on down, then.'

They went most of the way down the hill-face in silence. Mr Godwin took the lead, but they went slowly. It was this same face she had seen him come down before, and she wondered more than ever at the virtuosity of it. At this pace he made it seem very easy. They did not go straight down, but he had an infallible eye for the right line. She had only one thing in her mind. She did not want to ask the question, but she knew that, at some point before they separated, she would ask it. They were almost down to the road when she said, 'What has she really got against Mr Macalister, then? Mrs Haskell, I mean.'

He went on ahead of her and spoke without turning round. 'Oh,' he said, 'hell hath no fury, I suppose, if the story's true. Admittedly, she did pretty well for herself, socially, I mean, marrying Haskell. But it's not the same as being the laird's leddy. She's a born climber, and the mother was no great shakes socially, from all accounts. I don't know about the father. No one ever saw him. That's one thing, certainly – pure social resentment. She may be the headmaster's wife, but she is still not received by the gentry. Things are pretty feudal up here, you know.'

'I know that. What's the other?'

'The other what?'

'You said the social resentment was one thing.'

He went for some time without answering. When they got down to the road, he turned and faced her. He looked at her with a sort of unwilling, clinical curiosity. 'I don't know, of course,' he said. 'Don't you think your guess is as good as mine? Maybe even better.'

She gave him back stare for stare. The warmth and ease was all gone, but there remained this curious sympathy between them, so that she did not really mind what he saw when he looked at her like that. 'That may be,' she said. 'But tell me your guess.'

He shrugged. There was no depth of feeling in him, but no vindictiveness either. 'All right,' he said. 'Straight sex. Whatever happened before, she's a married woman now, and she's married to Haskell. And there's Macalister, still around, still unattached. She's too goddamned respectable to have another go at him, even if he'd play, but that doesn't mean she doesn't still want him. So she takes it out in hate. It's common enough, surely.'

Kate nodded. 'Oh yes,' she said, 'common enough. You don't think much of your headmaster's wife, do you? There have been times when I have felt sorry for her.'

He said very deliberately, 'There's no harm in feeling sorry for her, so long as you don't let pity govern your actions. I agree, I don't think she's happy. I think she's pretty pure poison, all the same.'

'Everything's pure up here,' she said. 'There's nothing to dilute it.'

He gave her a small quick smile, but there was no cheerfulness in it. 'I'm afraid that's true,' he said. 'So long as you understand that. If you can't live with it, the only thing to do is get away.'

She said, 'How can I get away?' but he only shrugged.

'I'll go ahead,' he said. 'You come at your own pace.' He turned and set off along the road in his neat effortless run, but this time she did not watch him go.

It was not the last she saw of him, even so. When she came to the bridge, he was standing on the road at the far end of it, talking to someone. There was a rather battered Land-Rover parked just beyond them, but she could not see anyone in it. The man he was talking to had his back to her, but she never had much doubt who it was. The tweeds and pulled-down cap were common form round here, but it was the stance that identified him. He stood, motionless and slightly crouched, staring up into Peter Godwin's face as they talked. It was Alec, all right. They made an odd pair and looked as thick as thieves. She could not see Alec's face, but Peter's whole face was contorted in his impish smile. Neither of them had seen her yet, but one at least of them must know she would be coming. She did not want to go past them at all, not as close as that, but the bridge gave her no choice. She remembered the little girl's terror of passing alone by a bunch of people talking together. It was generally boys or men, but even women could do it, if they were women of an unfamiliar sort. There was always the moment when they would stop talking and turn their heads and look at her, and she could never make up her mind whether to look at them or not. If she looked at them, they might talk to her, and she did not want that. If she went by with head averted they might talk about her, or worse still laugh, or even call out to her, and then she would not know what to do. It was being alone when they were together that was the trouble. Nobody on his own ever frightened her.

She went on over the bridge, stepping out resolutely. She hoped they would not see her until she was almost past them. Then Peter Godwin lifted his face and saw her, and Alec, following his eyes in the quick, animal way he had, turned and saw her too, and they both stood there, looking at her as she came over the bridge. Both faces were smiling. They had already been smiling when they turned. They were not smiling at her, but at something they had already had between them before she came along. They were so enormously different, the one so civilised and the other so primitive, but it was the difference they had in common. They shared their lack of ordinary humanity and of any ordinary masculinity that she could command allegiance from. She went on walking and they went on smiling, but she did not think, even now, that they were smiling at her. They terrified her, standing there like that, but because the social rule required it, she formed her face into a small, recognising smile.

She was quite close to them before Peter Godwin's face changed. It was difficult to say how it changed, but now his smile was at least answering hers. At the same moment Alec raised his hand and lifted his cap. The normal social balance was restored, but inside herself she was still frightened. Peter Godwin did not say anything. She did not want him to say anything. For him to say good evening, as if he had not seen her before, would make them somehow conspirators, while to admit that he had seen her would be worse. But in this at least he was to be trusted. He nodded, and Alec said, 'Good evening, Mistress Wychett,' and she said good evening pleasantly to the pair of them and went on past them towards the school gate. She wondered whether it would ever be possible to get back into an ordinary way of feeling and behaving.

The sun was gone now, hidden behind the clouds westward, and the glen was full of dusk. It was always full of something. It was only on the tops that she felt free to breathe. If you could not live with it, Peter had said, the only thing you could do was to get away from it. For the first time she let herself wonder whether she could in fact do that. But she walked on steadily towards the house, where she would spend the evening sociably with Richard, knowing that she had arranged to go out next morning to the Corrie Dorcha to meet James.

He said, 'Well, how did it go?'

'All right, I think. He's very professional about it. No, professional isn't quite the word. But sort of neutral. There was none of the embarrassment you expect with amateur photography. He might have been photographing a mountain, almost.'

'Yes, I know what you mean. Anyway, he seemed pleased?'

'I think so. But let's see how they turn out. He didn't say when they'd be ready to have a look at.'

Richard laughed. 'You won't be shown a rough, I can tell you that. He'll get the job finished as he wants it before he lets anyone see it, even us. He's a bit of a prima donna over his photography. He's got his darkroom and all the rest up at his house, and I don't think anyone's ever allowed to see him at work.'

'Where does he live, in fact?'

'Well, a bit up the hill from here. Up behind the Haskells'.'

'By himself?'

'Oh yes, indeed. Some of the staff share, of course, but there are plenty of houses to go round. He wouldn't want to share, I imagine. For one thing, it would beg too many questions, and he's nothing if not careful. For another, he's quite the little housekeeper, I'm told. Everything just so. No bachelor snuggery with club armchairs and cigarette ash for him. He gets away with it because there's nothing soft about him. He's got a sharp mind and an edge to his tongue, and of course physically he can run rings round any of them. There's nothing for anyone to get hold of, not even the boys. They eat out of his hand. He's quite a formidable character, is Master Godwin.'

'Yes,' said Kate. 'Yes, I think he is. I like him, but he frightens me a bit.'

Richard looked at her. 'There's nothing for you to be frightened of,' he said. 'You mustn't expect to be able to manage him, because he's not subject to your sort of management. But equally he's got nothing he can use against you. As you say, neutral. And I agree, better that way. He's not a chap I'd like to be on the wrong side of.'

They left it at that, but the two figures at the end of the bridge would not go out of her mind, or the two faces turned to her, smiling, but not at her. It was not specifically malice, or if it was, she did not think it was directed against her. It was a sort of monstrous, jeering uninvolvement, as if they knew everything but felt nothing, except of course amusement at what they knew. She did not know what they could do to her, but she was still certain she had been right to be frightened.

Later she said to Richard, 'What do you think John Haskell really feels about his Janet?'

He took his eyes from his book and looked at her, eyebrows raised. He said, 'What does Godwin say?'

'All right, you win. But I haven't been gossiping with the staff. It's just that you can't stop him talking. Especially if you're being photographed. But I didn't join in.'

He nodded. 'What does he say, anyway?'

'He said she came as temporary secretary and nobbled him in six weeks. He assumes it was a matter of straight sex appeal.'

'Mm. I haven't been gossiping with the staff either, but I believe, as a matter of history, that is more or less what happened. I can't answer for his reasons. He's a lonely sort of chap, I think.'

'But is she all that attractive?'

He considered this with perfect gravity. 'I wouldn't use the word attractive,' he said, 'because there is so much about her that repels one. Me, anyhow. But simply as a body she's all right. And for all her pretensions, I think she's pretty keen. Put it like this: I think if I was stuck with her on a desert island, I'd soon find myself in bed with her. That's if we had a bed, of course. But I think after a bit I'd either murder her or hang myself from the nearest palm tree.'

'But he hasn't reached that point yet?'

He shook his head. 'I think he's got an enormous capacity for keeping himself to himself.'

They looked at each other with a sudden, curious solemnity. 'More than you?' she said.

'Much more than me.'

She got up. 'I'm tired,' she said. 'I think I'll go to bed.'

He nodded and went back to his book. 'You go on,' he said. 'I shan't be long.'

XII

He was standing under the rock waiting for her as she came up the path. There was no mist on the hill this time, only yellow sunshine in the still, chilly air. Ahead and on both sides of her the hill-faces ran up to the cloudless sky, and behind her the corrie flattened out in a long curve that framed the distant southern hills. Only the burn made any sound, and she and the burn were the only things that moved. He never took his eyes off her, nor she, more than she could help, off him. His face looked watchful, even apprehensive. She could not tell what he was thinking at all.

She was quite close to him before he moved. Then he came a pace or two to meet her, quite slowly, with his hands outstretched, and she put her hands in his, and they stood there, with only their hands touching, looking at each other. He said, 'Catriona, Catriona,' but very quietly, almost as if he was talking to himself. She said nothing, but the longing that welled up in her was so immense that her eyes filled suddenly with tears, so that she could no longer see him clearly. She blinked them away and felt them run cold down her cheeks as she looked up at him. His hands closed hard on hers, and he said, 'Oh, for God's sake,' almost savagely.

She pulled a hand free and found a handkerchief and mopped her face. He still held the other hand. She smiled at him. 'Sorry,' she said. 'But don't worry. I've never been so happy in my life.' But even as she said it, she knew that whatever it was she felt, it was not happiness. Part of her mind still hung helplessly over the abyss. She pulled the other hand free. 'Come on,' she said. 'Sit down and tell me what sort of a person you really are. I don't know anything about you. That's the extraordinary thing, don't you see? I don't really know anything about you at all. Nor you about me.'

She went away from him and sat down on a rock above the burn. After a moment he came and sat down beside her. He said, 'Is that what you came to say?'

She did not look at him now. She watched the burn running cold and clear between its boulders. It was only a trickle now compared with what it had been before. 'No,' she said, 'it's not.'

'Then what did you come to say?'

A wave of appalling hopelessness engulfed her. She knew what she had to say, but she knew that she could neither say it nor, ultimately, leave it unsaid. She did not want to say anything at all, only to sit there with him in the yellow sunlight and not have to make up her mind. 'Come on,' he said, 'better get it over with.'

'All right. I came to tell you that I was in love with you, but that the thing couldn't go on. I thought – I didn't know, but I thought you were in love with me. I thought you must be, for me to feel like that. I thought if we both knew where we were, we could agree never to say or do anything more about it. But we had to know. Or I had to, anyhow.'

He said, 'That was what you came to say. Are you still saying it?'

'I suppose so. What else is there to say? I love you more than I thought I could ever love anyone. I've no idea why. I love you whether you love me or not. But I'm married to Richard, and there doesn't seem anything I can do about it. We can't just have an affair. Here of all places. Anyhow, it wouldn't be any good.'

'Why wouldn't it be any good? I want it more than I've ever wanted anything. You talk about love. I'm not sure

110

about that. Perhaps I'm not up to it. All I know is that you've played hell with my peace of mind ever since I got out of the train and saw you standing there on the platform. No one's ever done that to me before. Whatever you call it, we've got something for each other we can't get from anyone else. Or so it seems. Why should we pass it up?'

'Because the chances are it's going to wreck my life if we don't. Is it going to wreck yours if we do?'

'Your life with Richard?'

'Yes, all right, my life with Richard. It's the only one I've got.'

'Are you sure it would wreck it?'

She said, 'That's the question I've been trying not to ask myself ever since I saw you. Because of course I knew what the answer was, and I couldn't face it. Yes, I am sure. I don't know what you make of Richard. I know him very well. For one thing he's very intelligent. Much too intelligent to be made a fool of. For another, if you see him as the *mari complaisant*, you'd better think again. He's kind and considerate and courteous, and of course he's quiet. But if he knew I was carrying on with you or anyone else, he'd fling me out at the drop of a hat.'

He took a breath as if he was going to say something, and she turned and looked at him. His face was drawn and desperately sad. She had never seen him look sad before, and it unnerved her, so that she had to press her arms to her sides to prevent herself from throwing them round his neck and trying to comfort him. He said, 'I don't much like the way you put it.'

'What,' she said, 'carrying on? But I mean that. I mean systematically deceiving him, having an affair, call it what you like. Trying to have it both ways, that's what it all comes to. It wouldn't work. It couldn't be done. Not with Richard. I'm telling you. I know him and you don't.' Her moment of softness had passed. She looked at him almost

111

fiercely. She said, 'You haven't answered my question.'

The sadness had gone from his face too. It seemed quite expressionless. 'What question?' he said.

'I said it might wreck my life if we had our affair. Would it wreck yours if we didn't?'

When he spoke, his voice was expressionless, too. It was as if he had suddenly withdrawn to an immense distance, and was considering the thing with complete detachment. 'I don't know,' he said. 'I don't know what it would do or what would happen. I've never found myself in this position before. That's a thing we shall have to find out.'

She turned on him with a touch of desperation. 'But we can't leave it like that, James,' she said. 'We can't just wait and see what's going to happen. It's too serious to experiment with.'

'No?' he said. He seemed to get blanker and blanker as she got more desperate. 'Then what can we do? You suggest some sort of joint act of renunciation. It wouldn't mean a thing, not when it came to the crunch. So long as we are both in the glen, the thing is going to be there, between us, and liable to explode at any time.' He looked away from her and seemed once more to be speaking as much to himself as to her. 'And if you left the glen,' he said, 'I believe I should follow you.' He turned and looked at her again, and seemed to take pity in her distress. 'Look, Catriona,' he said, 'it's no good my saying I'll give you up, just like that. I couldn't do it. If the occasion served and you were willing, we should make love. I'm not stating an intention. I'm stating a fact, or what seems to me a fact. But I promise you this. I won't' – he waved a hand, a little savagely, looking for the right words – 'I won't try to make the opportunity.' He smiled suddenly. 'I won't try to seduce you, force my vile attentions on you, try to break down your resistance.' He stopped smiling and looked at her, hard and direct. 'But that's the most I can promise. I'm sorry if this seems like putting the burden on you, but it isn't really. As I see it, we're on a level footing. I'm only trying to be realistic about it.'

For what seemed a very long time neither of them moved or spoke. The burn chattered quietly among the rocks, and an enormous bird floated over them on set wings, interested in their very stillness. He looked up, following it with his eyes. 'Buzzard,' he said. 'We have got a pair of eagles, but they're mostly farther up.' She still felt moved to protest, but was checked by the fear of seeming importunate, the old, resentful apprehension of the male assumption of greater reasonableness. All the same, she could not bring herself to explicit acceptance. Her mind beat round indignantly in the silence, looking for line of attack, and all the time conscious of a mounting physical tension, so that if she did not say something quickly, their bodies might simply take charge.

She said, 'Tell me about the holiday camp.' He let his breath go audibly, but did not move.

'What about it?' he said.

'It's awful,' she said. 'How could you bring yourself to do it? That's one of the things I don't understand about you.'

He moved then. He got up and went a few paces down to the very edge of the water, and stood there, looking down at it. He said, 'It was that or the place. We were broke. What would you have done?'

'But your father wouldn't sell.'

'You mean he didn't sell. No, he didn't. He had his own reasons. He left it to me to do it. But it was his doing we were in the mess we were. I can assure you I had no say in the way the place was run.'

'How was it run, then?'

'Oh – nothing dramatic. Just steady over-spending. He had great ideas of what was due to his position. Staff, entertaining, a general keeping up of appearances, even subscriptions, and for years mostly on borrowed money. We were in the red up to our eyebrows. Something had to go, and Cotton's was offering a price that would just about put us in the clear.' He turned and came back and stood looking down at her. He said, 'In point of fact, it hasn't done all that harm to the glen. I expect you've heard the worst made of it. But I think you should examine your witnesses' credentials.'

'You mean Janet Haskell? Yes, I know you turned her mother out, which gives her a special grievance.'

'I didn't, in fact, turn Janet's mother out. She left. But the point's unimportant. I am only suggesting that Janet may not be the most reliable guide in the matter. Or in any matter, if it comes to that. Anyway, that was the position. I repeat, what would you have done?'

She did not like the way he used the name. It was only a small thing, but it jolted her badly. She herself had talked of Janet Haskell. Sometimes she and Richard had called her our Janet, as a sort of euphemism. She could not think of her simply as Janet. It was like getting too close to her, and there was this repellent quality which Richard had noted. Yet to James, apparently, she was Janet, a person you could get that close to. But then he had got close to her, if the whisper in the glen was true. She remembered the mental horrors of her drive back from Aberwhinnie. Conjunct and bosomed with her, as far as we call hers. It was like a nightmare she had talked herself out of but could not quite forget. She looked up at him standing there in front of her, and was appalled, once more, at the strength and confusion of her own feelings.

Instead of answering his question she said, 'If it's any comfort to you, I wouldn't, for choice, believe anything Mrs Haskell said about anyone. I don't like her.' Janet Haskell had set her mouth and said, 'I don't like the man.' Nobody liked anyone in the glen, and they all went round telling each other so. She got up and found herself face to face with him, and a moment later his arms were round her body and hers were round his neck. His mouth came down on hers, and her legs would almost have gone from under her if he had not taken most of her weight. If he had been content only to kiss her, she might have melted irretrievably, but his hands began to work on her, groping under her clothes, and the horror of her imaginings came back into her mind. She turned her face away and tried to push her body clear of his. For a moment he held her by force, and they struggled, breathing fiercely like wrestlers interlocked. Then he let her go, and she plumped down, in sheer physical weakness, on to her rock and sat there again, looking up at him as he stood over her. She said, 'No, no, no,' almost in a whisper.

His face was full of anger and frustration. He said, 'What in God's name's the matter with you?' but she could not tell him, not now. She must have it out with him some time, but not now. All she wanted now was time. He must give her time. Surely he could give her time. It did not seem much to ask.

She said, 'I'm sorry, James, I'm sorry. But you said you'd leave it to me. You promised, do you remember? Not now. Please, not now.'

He yielded at once. To the wicked part of her mind, which would not altogether keep quiet, there was ever something adroit and practised in it, as if he was playing her, letting her have more line. He would be a fly-fisherman as well as a stalker. The anger went out of his face and he managed a rueful smile. He said, 'I wasn't contemplating rape, exactly. I thought you wanted it. But all right, it's for you to say.'

She put her head on her hands and saw the pebbles and rough grass under her feet through tears of misery and something very like humiliation. She said, 'Oh dear God, I want it. But give me time. Please give me time.'

He stooped and took her gently by the shoulders and got her to her feet. 'Come on,' he said, 'you'd better be on your way home,' and for the second time that morning she blinked her tears away and mopped her face fiercely, with a handkerchief which this time was already damp and cold in her pocket.

'Yes,' she said. 'You go straight up your way. There's no need for you to come with me at all. I shan't get lost today.' She was desperate to get away from him now, as desperate as she had been to come to him. And would be again. She had no doubt about that at all, but for the moment she was conscious only of an enormous relief that nothing final had happened and an overwhelming desire to be alone. She needed to think, about herself and about James, and when he was there she did not seem able to think at all.

He smiled at her. There was kindness in the smile, but she suddenly had the feeling that he knew exactly what was in her mind. This was something new and disconcerting that she had not reckoned on. She had grown used to the belief that Richard, with all his intelligence, did not know what she was thinking, and it had never occurred to her that with James she might be on any other footing. Now she suspected that she was, and it increased her already desperate vulnerability. He said, 'All right, Catriona. Off you go, then. I'm not going to ask when I shall see you again. But I shall, of course.'

She said, 'Oh yes, you will,' and he laughed outright.

'Don't sound so desperate about it,' he said. He took her by the arm and turned her to face down the path. She could find nothing to say to that. She made a gesture with the hand that still held the damp handkerchief and set off walking. She did not know how long he stood and watched her go, but this time she did not turn and look back.

Something in his attitude galled her, but she had an

uneasy feeling that he was being more honest than she was. Or perhaps rather that he was being more honest with her than she was being with herself. It had not been fair to say that they were on an equal footing, because she had so much more to lose. But that apart, she wondered whether there was any real difference in what they were doing to each other. She had said she loved him, and he had said she was playing hell with his peace of mind. Love sounded better. It remained possible that he might know more about these things than she did.

The sky was still clear, and the sun was warm on her face as she went down the path. The buzzard had lost interest in them when they moved, and was nowhere in sight. When the path left the burn, its quiet voice died away almost at once, and after that there was no sound anywhere but the occasional crunch of her feet on gravel. The southern hills swam in a blue translucent haze, and there was nothing in all the enormous landscape to show that man existed. The peace of the place began to work on her, reinforcing the relief she had brought from up the hill. When she came over the brow, the road was empty of traffic, and when the school buildings came in sight, she faced them with confidence. There were minds at work there, hostile minds, or curious, amused minds, or merely minds that had a legitimate interest in what she did. But they had nothing on her yet. For the moment, at least, she felt once more mistress of herself and able to defy the lot of them. There was more comfort than logic in it, but it was comfort she needed, and she did not stay to examine it too closely.

XIII

She was alone in the house when the telephone rang, and this time she could hardly bring herself to answer it. She still did not want to be involved again with anybody. She wanted to consolidate the mood she had brought down from the hill the day before, to turn in on herself and mend her own mind. The clear weather had gone, and it was raining gently again, but even this helped. She felt shut into the dark house, and liked the feeling. And now the phone was ringing in the hall, and whoever it was, she did not want to speak to them.

She opened the door into the hall, and the ringing became louder and more insistent. She stood there in the doorway, looking at the phone. It seemed odd that a completely motionless object could create such a disturbance. It went on ringing. There was a persistence in it, as if whoever was ringing knew she was there, and was daring her to come out of her hiding-place. The trouble was that they probably did. They would know that she had had no breakfast, and that she was there in the hall, watching the phone ring and hoping it would stop. There was no way of escape, not in this place. She walked across the hall with deliberate slowness and picked up the receiver. It was Mrs Haskell.

She said, 'Hullo? I am not disturbing you?' The now familiar Highland question, that was more than half a statement.

Kate said, 'Oh, hullo.' With any other caller, she would have added their name, but with Janet Haskell she could not do it. To say 'Mrs Haskell' would sound almost provocatively formal, and she would not and could not call her

Janet. 'No,' she said. 'I'm sorry I was so long coming. I had flour on my hands and had to wash them.' Another of those complete and deliberate lies on a matter of no possible importance.

'Oh well,' said Mrs Haskell, 'I thought you would not be out walking in this weather.' Kate thought, damn the woman, but said nothing. 'I was wondering,' said Mrs Haskell, 'would you come round and have coffee with me? I should like it if you would.'

Not quite the royal command, but the form of words galled her, all the same. Perhaps she was getting over-sensitive to the way people said things. Anyhow, there was no escape. She had known there would not be, and there was not. She said, 'Oh – yes. Yes, thank you, I'd like to.' What else was there to say? She would not be driven out of common form because other people failed to observe it. 'May I finish what I'm doing and come in half an hour?'

Mrs Haskell said, 'That would be fine. I'll expect you, then.'

'Right,' said Kate. They said goodbye and rang off. Kate went into the kitchen and got out the things for making pastry. She felt trapped by even her pointless, instantaneous lie. If she did not use flour for something, Mrs Haskell would have a way of finding out. She made her pastry, concentrating her mind deliberately on what she was doing. She put it in the refrigerator and put the things away and washed her hands, washing off the lie with the flour. The half hour was nearly up. She went into the hall and put on her waterproofs. She looked back at the dark privacy of the house with an almost desperate longing, but it was no use. She opened the door and went out into the rain.

When she came to the Haskells' house, Mrs Haskell was watching for her. Mrs Haskell was always on the watch. She opened the door and said, 'There you are,' as if she had half expected her not to come.

'Here I am,' said Kate. It seemed completely meaningless, but she did not know what else to say. She assumed that Mrs Haskell would say what she wanted to say, and that she would answer as best she could. Her attitude of mind was entirely passive and defensive. She had nothing to say herself, not to this woman. All the same, she found herself looking at her with a new, unwilling interest, as the other half of her hated fantasy. Mrs Haskell was dressed for the occasion. She must be. She had on a clinging, shiny frock with little frilly touches, which no one in her senses would wear for a wet morning at home. The shoes on her long, well-shaped feet were shiny, too. She led the way into the speckless, characterless sitting-room, and Kate observed with a sort of distasteful admiration how her opulent bottom swung as she walked. You know what men are. There was a coffee percolator bubbling steadily on the tiled hearth. You could tell from the smell that the coffee had been expensive but had now been stewed till it was undrinkable. The china was expensive, too, with flowers on it. Mrs Haskell played the headmaster's wife for all it was worth, and got it all wrong. She switched off the percolator, and Kate listened with an almost physical relief as the tortured liquid stopped glugging and settled back into the bottom of the pot.

Mrs Haskell said again, 'You're not out walking today,' half a question and half a statement, and Kate said, 'No.'

'You walk a lot. You're a great walker.'

'Yes,' said Kate, 'I like it.' This was going to be even worse than she had thought. She wondered whether to go over on to the offensive and start a topic of her own, but she could not think of anything to say. She never could with Mrs Haskell. She compromised by keeping the topic but asking a question herself. 'Do you not walk yourself?' she said. 'It's wonderful walking country, and there's not very much else to do, is there?'

'Oh, I walk,' said Mrs Haskell. 'But I have plenty else to do, of course.' The headmaster's wife again. Kate was tempted to ask what she did have to do, but decided to accept the rebuke meekly. 'Of course,' she said.

They got through the routine questions about how she liked her coffee, and Kate took her cup and sipped it. It was exactly as she had known it would be. Mrs Haskell was looking at her expectantly. 'I get my coffee sent up from Edinburgh,' she said. 'There's nothing much to be had in Aberwhinnie.'

'No?' said Kate. 'It's very good.' This at least was not wholly untrue. Wherever it had started from, the coffee had been good enough when it had fetched up at Glenaidon.

The attack came so suddenly and from such an unexpected quarter that it took her completely by surprise. Mrs Haskell put down her cup and said, 'Mr Godwin has been taking your photograph, I think.' It was impossible to tell whether she was trying to confirm her own suspicions or stating an acknowledged fact, but either way it made their innocent precautions seem very silly. Still, innocent they had been. There was nothing here that called for hedging.

Kate smiled brightly into her coffee cup. 'Yes,' she said, 'yes, he took some the other day. I haven't seen them yet. I gather he's a great photographer. Richard says some of his things are very good.'

She looked at Mrs Haskell, and her smile withered under the naked resentment of the fierce green eyes. Mrs Haskell said, 'Your husband did not mind?' She was full of a sort of triumphant disappointment.

Kate revived her smile and clamped it firmly on her face. She even managed a small laugh. She felt slightly sick. 'Mind?' she said. 'Good gracious, why should he mind? He thought it was quite a compliment.'

'Oh, that it may be. He certainly hasn't asked to photograph me.' There was a monstrous kittenishness in it, and for a moment Kate was taken aback, as she had been before, by a stab of pure feminine pity. Then she remembered Peter Godwin saying, 'Make a wonderful nude, wouldn't she?' and her fantasy came back over her, swamping her spurt of sympathy in physical disgust.

She took up Mrs Haskell's playfulness with a woman-to-woman smile. She said, 'I don't expect he'd dare. He probably thought you wouldn't like it.'

'I would not. A man like that. I don't think we ought to have him here.'

Kate was all innocence now. 'Oh?' she said. 'I thought he was good at his job. At least, I know Richard thinks so.'

'That's as may be. Do you not know what kind of a man he is?'

Dear God, thought Kate, even that she resented. Even that she took as a personal affront to her terrible femininity. She said, 'Really, Mrs Haskell, it is no concern of mine what sort of a man he is. Obviously I don't know him well, but I find nothing to dislike in him. And you know, I did meet him here, in your house.'

Mrs Haskell said, 'That was my husband's wish.'

'But surely if he was any sort of corrupting influence, your husband wouldn't have him in the school, let alone in his own house. Anyhow, I repeat, it's no concern of mine. Nor can I see why I should not allow him to take photographs of me if he wishes to, and if my husband has no objection. But if for any reason the thing upset you —'

'Oh, there was no question of my being upset. I was not supposed to know, you can be sure of that. But when I see Peter Godwin sneaking out with his camera and all, and – Oh well, maybe the thing is better left.'

Kate said, 'And me sneaking out after him?' She could not forgive the fact that it was true. That was just what she had done. Unduly tortuous, Richard had said, and she had defended Peter Godwin's discretion. What use was discretion in a place like this?

Mrs Haskell said, 'I did not say that.'

Kate put down her cup. She had not tasted it again. The coffee was disgusting, anyway. She said, 'Mrs Haskell, Mr Godwin suggested taking the photographs. He discussed it with me and with my husband, and I discussed it with my husband. He asked me to meet him at a particular place he had in mind for the purpose, and I did. He took the photographs, and we came back. If you find anything' – she hesitated, discarded a stronger word, and said – 'anything questionable in that, I can only suppose it is your – your way of looking at things that makes you find it so.' She would not be dragged into the gutter, certainly not into a gutter of Mrs Haskell's making. It occurred to her when it was too late that for her to behave like a lady only aggravated her offence. Whatever the state of her seething mind, Mrs Haskell had no social defences, and to expose anyone's defencelessness was never wise. It would have been better to answer her like a fishwife, only she could not bring herself to do it. It would be like laying violent hands on a physically filthy opponent. If you could not fight them at a distance, there was nothing for it but to turn and run.

All the same, she could not have anticipated the effect of her attack. Mrs Haskell put her cup down very slowly, watching it all the way, because the hand that held it was shaking. Her face was flooded with colour and her eyes were clouded. Then she keeled over sideways on to the arm of her chair and put her head on her hands and started to cry. She cried, as she did everything, with a sort of monstrous suppressed violence that was altogether horrifying. The chair creaked under the shaking of the great shining shoulders, but she did not make a sound. Kate sat there and watched her, utterly at a loss. She wanted only to get up

123

and take her things and run, but she knew she must not. She had to see the thing out. All the same, there was nothing she could say, because what she had said could not be retracted and called for no apology. She knew, with the sharp intelligence of guilt, that it was not in being photographed by Peter Godwin that her real offence lay. But her real offence could not be mentioned. Apart from anything else, it existed, so far, only in Mrs Haskell's imagination. And in her own, of course. There was nothing she could do about that, either. She sat there, waiting for the storm to subside and wondering, with a cold crawling apprehension, what would emerge when it did.

Gradually the convulsive sobbing stopped. Mrs Haskell still kept her face down on her hands, so that Kate could not see it, but the red flush died out of the bent neck. She breathed short and quick, as if she had been running. When at last she spoke, her voice was very quiet but very clear. She said, 'Look what you do to me between the lot of you.' Whatever the real offence, it was her dignity and self-esteem that was upset now. She was the headmaster's wife, reduced to tears by the unanswerable anger of the wife of one of her husband's staff. The flowered china and the coffee from Edinburgh were no use to her now.

Kate was conscious again of that appalled and appalling pity, with its undercurrents of revulsion and even straight fright. She took breath to speak, but could not find the words she wanted. Mrs Haskell sat suddenly upright and stared at her, waiting for her to say something. Her eyes were wide and wet, but there were no tears on her cheeks. Kate said, 'Mrs Haskell —' and stopped.

Mrs Haskell said, 'Can you not call me Janet?'

Of herself she could not, but under this pressure she had no alternative. 'Janet, then,' she said, 'nobody's doing anything to you. Or I am not, at least. Why should I?'

'Are you not?' She still spoke very quietly, as if she was considering the thing in her own mind rather than looking for an answer from Kate. And as if she did not want to interrupt what was going on in the other woman's mind, Kate shook her head but said nothing.

Mrs Haskell looked away from her, staring into a far corner of the room. Quite suddenly, she smiled, and then, very slowly, turned the smile on Kate. It was an odd, incommunicative smile, but Kate was conscious of immediate relief. Mrs Haskell smiling she could deal with. Mrs Haskell weeping she could not deal with at all. 'Ah well,' said Mrs Haskell, 'what else is there you could say?'

Kate's moment of pity had passed. There was no harm in feeling pity for Mrs Haskell, so long as you did not let it govern your actions. That was another thing Peter Godwin had said, and he missed nothing. She said, 'What indeed?' She said it quite lightly. She was determined to de-fuse the whole explosive situation and get away as fast as she could. She said, 'I'd better be going, hadn't I? You'll want time to get over your upset.' She made it sound quite kind, but she was ruthlessly determined. There must be no explanations. Above all, no explanations. The unmentionable thing that lay between them must lie there still, still unmentioned. As to those damned photographs, she must warn Peter Godwin. At all costs she must get hold of him and tell him something at least of what had happened. Otherwise Mrs Haskell would raise the thing with him first, and she did not like to think what they would make of it between them if she did. She got up, and Mrs Haskell sat looking at her for a moment, and then got up too. Get the thing on to a social level, and she was always manageable.

She said, 'Well, if you think so. It's a pity —' She broke off and moved towards the door. As she went, she said, 'I don't have many people to talk to, and that's a fact.'

She was angling for pity now. She knew it had been there, and she wanted it back. The fact itself was in a way pathetic, but Kate's pity was exhausted. She said, 'No, it's not a big place, is it?' She spoke, again, lightly, almost cheerfully. The headmaster's wife always had plenty she must do. She would not throw it at her direct, but she did not think she could forget it.

Mrs Haskell had no weapons for this sort of fencing. She went out into the hall, saying nothing. It was exactly as it had been at Kate's house, only this time it was Kate who put on her waterproofs in the silence. She opened the front door herself. Mrs Haskell just stood there, watching her. Common form demanded that something further be said, but Kate was not going to say it until she was outside the door. When she was, she said, 'Well, thank you for the coffee. I'm sorry you got upset. I didn't mean to upset you.' It was true, as far as it went, and it met the immediate requirements.

Mrs Haskell said, 'Oh well, maybe I upset too easily,' and they said goodbye, and Kate went off down the path. She had gone some way when she heard the door shut behind her. She walked on, neither too fast nor too slow, until she was out of sight round the end of the house. Then she all but ran.

She wondered where Peter Godwin was. In the school, presumably, at this hour. No one could get at him there. She wondered whether he went back to his well ordered house for lunch. Almost certainly not. She might try to phone him there, in case. Failing that, she considered the possibility of going up and leaving him a note, but she had an instinct to put nothing on paper. There was Richard, too. Richard was in on this, superficially, but it was not the superficialities that mattered, and she did not like the implications. A much watered down version, perhaps. He had no means of finding out more than she told him. But Peter Godwin was the urgent thing. She hurried up the hill and let herself into the house. It was still dark and quiet, with the rain falling outside, but now she found no refuge in it.

XIV

Richard did not come back for lunch. She tried phoning
Peter Godwin's house, but he had not come back either.
She did not suppose Mrs Haskell could get at him so long
as he was at the school. She must try to get hold of him
when he came back in the evening. If he came back before
Richard, she could still phone him, but she did not want to
tell Richard about the thing now, or at least not until she
had spoken to Peter. The more she thought about the morning, the more it horrified her, but the horror was one she
had to keep to herself and would not find it easy to conceal.
With Peter it did not matter. He knew what was involved.

She spent a restless and miserable afternoon. The rain
was still falling outside. She knew that the best thing she
could do was to go out walking in it, but she could not bring
herself to do it. Even her walking was circumscribed now.
She could go out behind the Haskells' house, but she had
the feeling that the house, like Mrs Haskell herself, had
eyes in the back of its head. She felt more and more
trapped, and did not know how long the thing could go
on.

She made herself tea early and drank it by herself in the
kitchen. She could make some more when Richard came in.
When she had finished, she washed the things up and put
them away. Even this she did not want to have to explain.
As soon as it seemed worth trying, she went into the hall
and dialled Peter Godwin's number. If she carried the receiver to the full length of its flex, she could just see out of
the hall window, so that if Richard came up the path, she
could go back and put the receiver down before he got to

the door. She stood there, peering round the side of the window, and listened to Peter's phone ringing in his empty house. She let it ring for quite a time. Then she made herself put the receiver down and wait. She waited five minutes by her watch, and then tried again. The phone rang at the other end and she went over to the window, pulling on the flex gingerly, so as not to have the phone off its table. Almost at once she saw someone on the path. She went back and put the receiver down, and then ran back to the window. It was not Richard at all. It was Peter himself.

She went to open the door to him, but thought this would not do. Instead she went back to the door of the sitting-room and stood there in the doorway, waiting for him to ring. He rang, and she went across to the door and opened it. 'Oh, Peter,' she said. 'Come in. I've been wanting to talk to you.'

He looked at her curiously. There was an odd, muted excitement in his eyes. 'Have you?' he said. 'What's the trouble?'

She led the way into the sitting-room. 'It's Mrs Haskell,' she said. 'I wanted to tell you before Richard gets in. I – I don't want him upset with it. Sit down.'

He sat, but only on the arm of the chair, so that as she sat his face was well above hers. 'What's she been up to now?' he said.

'It's only that she knows about the photos. I think she guessed. Anyway, she asked me to go down and see her this morning, and put it to me direct. I saw no reason to deny it, of course. But it was all a bit horrible. I don't think she's quite sane, Peter.'

He thought about this. 'No?' he said. 'You may be right. Myself, I'd say bad rather than mad. But either way, I agree, dangerous to know. By the way, Richard won't be back for a bit. He's got caught up. Tell me what happened.'

She told him as much as she could bring herself to tell.

129

'The thing is,' she said, 'I think she'll probably have a go at you about it, and I wanted you to know before she does. My guess is that she'll want to see them.'

He smiled down at her. 'Over my dead body,' he said.

'But why, Peter? It really will make less trouble if you let her see them. Then she can't feel – excluded, do you know? I'm not saying it's reasonable. But anything rather than give her a fresh grievance. And after all, what harm can it do? They're only ordinary portraits. Otherwise she'll build the whole thing up in her mind.'

He shook his head. 'They're mine,' he said. 'I can't stand the woman, and I won't have it.'

She looked up at him, a little helplessly. She had no influence over him of any sort. He answered to no ordinary rules, and he could not be managed. That had been Richard's phrase. She could not expect to manage him, because he was not susceptible to that sort of management. She wondered, in passing, what Richard knew of her powers of managing other men, but Peter Godwin was the immediate problem. She said, 'It's no good asking you, as a personal favour, to let her see them if she asks?'

She was aware, as she said it, that she was asking a Highland question herself now. She made a question of it, but she knew in her own mind that it was no good. Peter Godwin shook his head, smiling at her with his odd, catlike smile. 'Afraid not,' he said. 'Would you like to see them? I've got them here.'

The truth was that she no longer wanted to see them. The mood of exaltation in which she had first faced the camera seemed infinitely remote. The photographs were just another burden, another strand in the net of guilt and deception which in this place seemed to weave itself round even her most innocent actions. All the same, she could not refuse, for fear of seeming piqued and unreasonable. She was curious too, of course. Not even her apprehensions could altogether stifle that. She wanted to see what this odd man and his camera had made of her. 'All right,' she said. Then, when this sounded too unenthusiastic, 'Yes, of course, I should like to.'

He took an envelope from the inner pocket of his jacket and opened it. There was a small pack of photographs inside, four or five of them. He pushed them across to her, watching her all the time. He did not say a word. She pulled her eyes away, almost with an effort, from the watchful, silent face hanging over her and looked at the top photograph.

In spite of herself, it moved her. There was a radiance in the face, even an innocence, which she longed to recognise but hardly dared to. It was like looking at a photograph of herself as a smiling child, and wondering in what possible sense this could be the same person as she now was. She remembered his saying, 'I only hope somebody's worth it,' and it came to her as she looked at it that after all no one was. She was not even worth it herself. She did not say anything. She looked at the photograph for a moment in silence. Then she shook her head and moved it to the bottom of the pack.

The next one was easier to deal with, because the face was not looking into the camera. It was a profile, with the hair blowing lightly across the face and the white background of distant mountains standing up in greater detail behind it. She could let herself admire it, critically and steadily, as she was used to admiring herself in the glass. She could admire the photography, too. The quality was unmistakable. Peter might be a bit a prima donna over his photography, but he was a marvellous photographer. It did not move her, as the first one had, but she could be proud of this one anywhere. Still no one said anything. She moved it down to the bottom and looked at the next.

This was disturbing in quite a different sort of way. The

eyes looked into the camera, but not quite at it. They were withdrawn and watchful, and the whole face was uneasy and indecisive. She knew this face, even if she had never seen it. It was herself as she now was. It did not startle or upset her, because she had already faced up to it in her mind. This was a portrait of Kate Wychett of Glenaidon, just as the first had been, God help her, a portrait of Catriona. She studied it long and critically before she moved it down and looked at the next.

It shook her, immediately and painfully, so that she tried to reject it as false, but could not. Once more the face looked into the camera, but here the eyes bored into you as you looked at them. It was a mask of hatred and disgust. She knew what the eyes were really looking at. She had looked at it too often in her mind's eye not to know that. Portrait of a jealous woman. Too good a portrait by half. She did not spend long on this one. As she shifted it, she heard Peter Godwin take a long breath, and a moment later she herself seemed to stop breathing altogether.

The fifth photograph was not a portrait at all. It was a landscape with figures. Or rather, part of a landscape. She had little doubt that what was printed here was only a comparatively small part of the original negative, but even brought up to this size it was full of detail. The black rock stood up just left of and a little above centre. Even when he was making this print, the photographer had not let himself forget the rules of composition. The figures were close by the rock, but not quite outlined against it. James had his back mostly to the camera, but her own face, tilted up to his, was immediately recognisable. Her arms were locked round his neck. His left arm, on the side nearer the camera, was close about the small of her back, pulling the lower part of her body in against his. His right arm and hand were invisible, but it was all too clear what they were up to. Her skirt was up almost round her waist. It was a slightly ridiculous, slightly pathetic scene, the sort of scene most people played out at some time in their lives, but no one would want overlooked, let alone photographed. She found herself shivering violently, and her heart thumped so that it must almost be audible in the silence. She moved the photograph quickly to the bottom of the pack, but could not face again the radiant innocence of the first. She put the whole pack down on the table in front of her, but could not bring herself to look up at Peter Godwin as he sat there above her.

When she spoke at last, her voice was a husky whisper. She said, 'Peter, how could you?'

He was a little breathless himself, but even without looking at him she could tell from his voice that he was smiling slightly. The tone was apologetic, but there was no softness in it. He said, 'I'm sorry. I didn't mean to, I promise you. I mean, I wasn't stalking you deliberately. I just came over the top, and there were these two bodies on the landscape. Wild life, you might say. I reacted instinctively. I flopped down in the heather and had my camera up without thinking about it. Then I waited to see what would happen. One does, you know. One wants to see what the creatures, left to themselves, are going to do.' He paused. 'They didn't, in fact, do much, did they? For the matter of that, if they had, I probably shouldn't have been able to get a photograph. But I couldn't resist this one.'

She still did not look up. She was flooded, not so much with shame as with self-disgust, because the thing, when you looked at it from the outside, was so sordid and ridiculous. As if he could watch her mind working, Peter said suddenly, 'Cheer up. I expect even Helen of Troy looked pretty silly with her legs in the air.'

She shook her head, as if to clear the picture out of it. She said, 'What are you going to do?'

'Do?' He sounded genuinely puzzled. 'I'm not going to

do anything. What should I do?'

She said nothing. She still had her eyes fixed on the table with its little pack of photographs. He said, 'You didn't imagine I was going to blackmail you or anything, did you? Why should I? When you come to think of it, what is there I want of you? More to the point, what are you going to do?'

She looked up at him at last. 'You mean, now someone knows?'

He almost snorted with impatience. 'My sweet fool,' he said, 'everyone knows. You can take that for granted. No details, of course. But everyone assumes there is something between you and Macalister. No one knows how far it has gone, but you know enough by now to be sure that they are not likely to underestimate the distance. To be honest, I was pretty startled myself when I saw you push him away. And disappointed, I suppose. But that's just the photographer in me. It wouldn't mean a thing to me otherwise.'

She said, 'But Richard —'

'Ah,' he said, 'Richard's the exception. No one will have said anything to Richard. If Richard knows anything, he knows it only from you. How much that may be you can judge better than I can.'

She nodded but did not say anything. When he spoke again, there was a touch of something like kindness in his voice. 'Look, Kate,' he said, 'it's not for me to advise you. And I don't suppose, in fact, it matters to me all that much what you do or what comes of it. But for what it's worth, don't be such a bloody fool.'

The door of the sitting-room was shut, but she heard Richard moving in the hall before he got to it. She was up out of her chair and half-way to the door when he opened it. He said, 'Oh, hullo.' His eye went past her. 'Hullo, Godwin,' he said. He walked straight past her towards the table. The pack of photographs still lay there. 'Ah,' he said, 'they're ready?' He stooped and picked them up and spread them fanwise in his hand. There were only three. Over his shoulder Peter Godwin looked at her with a blank expressionless stare.

She suddenly knew what was going to happen. She said, 'I'm sorry —' and flung herself out of the door and across the hall to the lavatory. She managed to shut the door behind her and got her head over the pan before she actually started to vomit.

As usual, the act of vomiting brought physical weakness but immediate emotional relief. She was mopping herself down at the wash-basin when Richard spoke from the other side of the door. He said, 'Are you all right?'

She spat out the water she had been rinsing her mouth with. She did it audibly, because she wanted to make plain the reality and extent of her physical distress. She said, 'Yes. Yes, I'm all right. Sorry it had to happen when Peter Godwin was here. Has he gone?'

'Yes.'

'Good. I'm just coming. I don't know what it was, but I'm all right now. Will you get yourself some tea? I'll see what I feel like.'

'All right,' he said.

She straightened herself up, looking at herself in the glass over the basin. She had seen that face before, quite recently. It would be one of the three faces waiting for her in the other room, unless Peter had taken them home with him. He had not. When she went into the sitting-room, there they were, still on the table. The profile was on top. Portrait of a lady. Then came the portrait of Kate Wychett. Catriona was at the bottom, but she hardly looked at her. She left them where they were and went into the kitchen.

Richard was just making the tea. He finished pouring the water into the pot before he looked at her. Then he said again, 'All right?'

She smiled at him. It was a wan smile, whatever that was. It was meant to show that she was herself again, but could not stand much of anything. 'Yes, thank you,' she said. 'Poor Peter. What a way of showing my gratitude.'

Richard said, 'Don't worry about Peter. Embarrassment is not in his nature. He made a joke of it, of course. Said he had never known his work received with such emotion, or something of the sort. Then he left the photos and took himself off before you need reappear. There's nothing wrong with his manners. What was it upset you, do you think?'

She shook her head. 'I don't know. I was summoned to have elevenses with our Janet. The coffee was terrible. So was she, for the matter of that. But I didn't think either of them was bad enough to make me actually throw up.'

'Were you? What did she want?'

'The awful thing is, I think she wants company. And Richard, I can't bear her. What am I to do?'

Something of her real distress came through her statement of a merely social dilemma. He looked at her, worried. She thought he was worried because he was facing for the first time since they had got here the possibility that she might not, after all, be finding the place tolerable. Then he decided to put the thing aside. He smiled. 'Don't drink her coffee, for a start,' he said.

She nodded and smiled back. She did not want to pursue the matter any more than he did. She said, 'What do you think of the photos?'

'Technically excellent,' he said. 'But then I expected that.' He put the tray down on the table. Then he went through into the sitting-room and came back with the photos in his hand. The portrait of a lady was still on top, and he was looking at it as he came in. 'That's a beauty,' he said. 'Don't you think so?'

'I do, yes. Much the nicest I've ever had taken. I mean –

modesty apart, it's such a lovely picture.'

He was looking at the next one now. Portrait of Kate Wychett. He looked at it long and carefully. 'This one's brilliant, too, in its way, but I can't say I like it awfully. What about you?'

She put on an expression of critical doubt. 'I'm not sure,' she said. 'It doesn't make such a nice picture. Is it like me?'

He nodded, still looking at the photograph. 'Oh yes,' he said. He looked at it again for a moment, but did not say anything more. Then he turned it over and looked at Catriona. He did not waste much time on her. 'That's a prettier picture,' he said. 'But it's not like you at all.'

XV

The rain must have stopped just before morning, and the sun came up a misted yellow on a world that glistened and ran with water. She said to Richard, 'I'm going into Aberwhinnie to shop. Anything you want?'

'Nothing really,' he said, 'but I'll think of something desperately urgent if you need it.'

'You mean in case our Janet summons me again? Don't worry. I'm going anyhow. One must shop, after all.'

'Think of something a bit personal,' he said. 'Tell her you've simply got to get some medicated powder and some mouthwash. Then she can enjoy herself wondering which of us has got false teeth and which of us has got athlete's foot, or whether one of us has got both, and if so, which. That should keep her busy for a bit.' He was determined to be spritely about Mrs Haskell now. That was because she had frightened him about her yesterday. It was as if by making a joke of her he could somehow neutralise the threat. Yet it was he who had said, after that first dinner party, that the woman was dangerous.

She shook her head, smiling. 'It won't do to provoke her,' she said. 'But don't worry. I am going shopping, and shopping I will go.'

'Good,' he said. 'What about the photos? Shall I give them back to Godwin? I imagine that's what he expects. Then I'd like to ask him for a couple of prints of the good one, when he can find time to do them. Do you agree?'

So it was to be the portrait of a lady. Well, what else could it be? She thought she knew what Peter's choice would have been, but she could ask him for a copy of that later. She had nothing more to hide from Peter. 'Yes,' she said, 'certainly. I'll never see myself to better advantage, so let's have it for the record.'

He nodded and put the photographs in his pocket. He had not been gone ten minutes before the phone rang. She went to it prepared, but it was Mrs Grant. 'I've been meaning to ring you,' she said, 'but you know how it is.'

Kate said she knew how it was.

'Anyhow, look, I was wondering, could you and Richard dine with us next Thursday? I was going to ask James —' Her voice trailed away slightly, and Kate came in sharp on her cue. 'Oh yes?' she said. 'Yes, that would be fun.'

She managed it perfectly, and Mrs Grant came in again with a sort of rushed relief. 'Oh good,' she said. 'I'm so glad. I tell you what. I'll write to you and tell you how to find us. One always has to up here the first time. But so long as I can count on you.'

'Yes, of course, we'd love it.'

There was a moment's pause, and then Mrs Grant said, 'I wish I could find an odd woman to square up the numbers, but one never can, not up here. That's half James's trouble, of course. I wish he'd find himself a wife and stop making trouble for everybody.' She gave a little laugh.

'Yes,' said Kate. 'Yes, so you were saying.'

'Yes, well, never mind. Perhaps I can think of someone. Anyway, I'll count on you for Thursday. And I'll write straight away and tell you how to get here.'

'That will be fine,' said Kate, and they said goodbye and rang off. She put the receiver down and wandered to the window. The sun shone bright outside, and she was pleased. She wanted to see James again, and she wanted to see him like that, in safe, neutral surroundings, where she could think about him clearly and things could not get out of hand. She wondered about Mrs Grant's odd woman. She hoped she would not be able to find her, or, if she did, that she would be very odd indeed. Meanwhile, the sun shone and she was still safe. Once she had come to terms with its existence, she found that she did not very much mind that photograph's being in Peter's hands. That was a part of his curious neutrality. It did not mean to him what it would have meant to other people, even what it meant to herself. It was a trophy of the chase, an unusual study of wild life taken unawares. He probably, in his impish, inhuman way, saw it as funny, but that was about all. And it was safe with him, because for all his inhumanity he was without malice. The fact, the memory, was there in her own mind, and the physical record of it was there in Peter's pocket, and both were equally safe. And whatever he said, no one else knew anything, because there was nothing else for anyone to know. Let them suspect what they liked. They would do that whatever she did. But nothing had happened. She went into the kitchen and started in on Richard's breakfast things. Then the phone rang again.

Because she had just settled with him comfortably in her own mind, his voice was a shock to her. He said, 'Catriona? It's James here. Are you free to talk to me, or must I be just social?'

She said, 'Oh, James. No, it's all right. I'm alone in the house. I suppose the line's all right?'

'Oh yes, it's an independent line, not through a switchboard or anything. Unless Janet's got her own private one installed. I wouldn't put it past her.'

Kate said, 'No.' The name had stung her again, and the way he spoke of her.

He did not seem to notice anything. He said. 'Look, I promised I wouldn't try to see you, and I'm not trying. I hear we're meeting at the Grants' on Thursday, but that doesn't count. We shan't be able to talk then, anyway. But I do want to talk to you. May I, please?'

She sighed. Pigeon-holing him neatly in a corner of her mind did not seem to do much good. She stood there, propped up against the wall, with her heart thumping and the receiver not quite steady in her hand. 'You seem to be doing it,' she said. 'Go on, then. What is it you want to say?'

He laughed, but he did not sound very cheerful. 'You're not very encouraging, are you?' he said. 'But I take a lot of discouraging where you're concerned. Look, Catriona, there's something worrying you, isn't there? All right, I know you've got plenty to worry about in general, but I don't mean that. There's something that – I don't know, gets in the way. Something you haven't said that sticks in your throat. What is it? I think you ought to tell me. I don't think it's fair not to.'

Fair, she thought, fair. A nice male word, that. Not cricket, not according to Cocker. In God's name, was it all a game, and if it was, who made the rules, anyway? She said, 'I'm sorry if you think I'm being unfair to you, James.'

He exploded suddenly over the phone. 'Damn it, Catriona,' he said, 'of course you're being unfair. I can't fence with you like this. I'm nearly out of my mind about you, can't you see that? I wander about the hill at night instead of sleeping decently in my bed, and then I have to get my things dry so that no one knows. I've got to keep up appearances, too, you know. For your sake as well as for my own.'

Her mind somersaulted again. She felt she really was being unfair to him, in one way if not in another. It was not a game after all. The thing had to be opened up and looked at, for both their sakes. She said, 'I'm sorry, James, I'm sorry. All right. There is something, you're quite right.'

There was a moment's silence. 'Go on,' he said.

'It's – it's the person you were just talking about.'

'Janet?'

'Her, yes. James – what was there between you and her, before she got married, I mean? I'm not just being bitchy. I'm not delving into your past. I don't mind about anyone else. But her I do mind about. She – she gives me the horrors, James. I can't stand the idea of it. I'm sorry.'

This time the silence was even longer. At last he said, 'And who's been feeding you that little bit of poison?'

'Oh, never mind. That doesn't matter, does it? Not she herself, anyway, you can be sure of that.'

'No,' he said. 'No, it wouldn't be. All right. Here it is, for what it's worth. It was before she married Haskell, as you say. Her mother lived in one of our cottages. Well, you know about that. She was away somewhere, being trained or doing a job or something. Anyway, I'd never seen her, or not to notice. I think I just about knew she existed. Then she came home to her mother's, and then of course I did see her. She took care I should. All red hair and curves out there in the front garden when I went past. We don't see many like that in the glen. You know that. Of course I got to know her. Anybody would.'

'Would they?'

'Yes, anybody. Even your Richard. Ask him, if you don't believe me.'

She surrendered. She said, 'All right. As a matter of fact, I have.'

'And what did he say?'

'He said that if he was on a desert island with her, he would find himself in bed with her pretty soon. But he thought that after a bit he'd either murder her or hang himself on a palm tree.'

He laughed. 'Good for him,' he said. 'Well, I wasn't on a desert island with her, and I didn't, so the question of murder or suicide didn't arise. But I know what he means, all right.'

'Then what did happen?'

He sighed. He said, 'Catriona, my dearest, if you aren't being a bitch, you're giving an awfully good imitation of one.'

She remembered Peter Godwin's fourth photograph, one of the two he had not left on the table. Portrait of a jealous woman. Portrait of a bitch would do as well. 'All right,' she said, 'I'm a bitch. I still want to know what happened.'

He said, 'All the best women are, a bit.'

'Never mind about my place in your personal ranking list. What happened, James?'

'Nothing happened. She made damned sure of that. It was wedding-bells or nothing for our luscious Janet. I suppose that's what poor old Haskell found, but I wasn't as mad as that. And she was as cunning as a snake. Not even her mother knew what was going on. Now there was an old bitch for you. But Janet played it very, very close to her chest.'

His voice wavered slightly, and she said, 'I don't like your choice of words. But go on.'

'Sorry. Just a manner of speaking. Anyway, I was still forcing my vile attentions on her, and she was still playing me for all she was worth, when we walked slap into my father. Or rather he walked slap into us. One day on the hill, that was. When I got home, we had a pretty well stand-up fight. Not only about that. About everything. We told each other a good many home truths, and I went south next day and got myself a job of sorts. I didn't come back till he was dead, and by that time she was Mrs Haskell. And that, I need hardly say, was the end of that.'

'On both sides?'

He was quiet for a bit, as if he was thinking what to say. Then he said, 'So far as Janet's concerned, she is the headmaster's wife, and she's not going to risk that. So far as I am concerned, you have my solemn assurance that I wouldn't lay a finger on Janet now in any circumstances, not on a desert island or anywhere else. So I'm one up on your Richard in that respect at least. Anyhow, as I say, the occasion wouldn't arise – not with Mrs Haskell as she now is. You must know that as well as I do. So that's it, Catriona. All right, I made a pass at her before, but nothing came of it. I shall never make a pass at her again. I don't want to, and in any case I shan't have the chance. So where does that leave me? If you're going to bar everyone who's found Janet Haskell physically attractive, you're going to find yourself in some pretty queer company.'

She was aware, perfectly clearly and simultaneously, of the fact that she was being talked over and of enormous relief that she could let him do it. In reason, his case was a good one. So far as physical events went, Janet Cameron had probably been one of the more innocuous pieces of his past. It was her own almost physical horror of the woman that was the trouble. She could not get over this, but now at least she could make a show of reason in keeping it apart from what she felt for James. She said, 'All right, James. I suppose I've been a fool about this. But it was rather sprung on me, and I couldn't help reacting. It's the effect she has on me.'

'Not a fool,' he said, 'just a bitch, and there's no great harm in that. So long as you don't treat me like a leper the next time we meet. Whenever that may be, even if it's only next Thursday.'

'I won't,' she said. 'And James – James, please don't go wandering about the hill at night. I can't bear that you should.'

'Not even if you wandered too?'

'How can I?' she said. 'That's why I can't bear your doing it. Can't you see?'

He said, 'Oh, Catriona. I do love you.'

She felt enormously serene and triumphant. She said,

'Do you, James? I thought I just played hell with your peace of mind.'

'Oh, what's the difference?'

'You're quite right. There isn't any. I came to that conclusion myself the other day. It's just that love sounds better. Anyway, I like to hear you say it.'

There was silence at the other end of the phone. Then he said, 'Have you walked up your side of the glen?'

'Above the school, do you mean? No, I never have. I don't know why.'

'Try it,' he said. 'One of these dark evenings. It gets dark early now. That way you won't have any bridges to cross.'

'What about you?'

'Oh, there's two sides to every glen and more ways of crossing the water than over the bridge.' He sounded suddenly very Highland.

'Ay,' she said, just. Ye'd best be wearing the kilt, maybe.'

He said, 'Oh God, Catriona, make it soon.' His voice sounded throaty and rather breathless.

'I'll try,' she said. 'Goodbye for now, James.'

'Goodbye, then, Catriona.'

She put the receiver down gently and leant back against the wall to steady herself. She was mad. That was all there was to it. Mad, and a bitch to boot. There did not seem to be anything she could do about it. She went into the kitchen to make out her shopping list. When she had finished, she did not put on her shopping clothes. Instead she went out of the house, just as she was, into the pale, chilly sunshine, and turned and went straight up the hill.

It was steeper than she expected. There was no house above theirs. There was a house a bit higher than theirs, but it was over to the right, above the back of the Haskells'. That would be Peter's. She went straight on up through the trees. She walked steadily for five minutes and saw clear hillside above. There was no path through the trees. The going was clear enough, but slippery with pine needles. At the edge of the trees she came to a path running sideways along the face. She turned right-handed along it, and came almost at once to a track that branched off it and went away up the face. It was the usual rough track, dodging between the boulders and the heather clumps. Animals had made it, and from the look of it it was still mostly animals that used it. She turned and went up it.

After a bit she stopped and looked back. She was clear of the line of the trees already. She could see the upper part of the school buildings and glimpses of the staff houses showing between the motionless pointed treetops. She could be seen now, if anybody was looking, but she was only going for a walk in the late autumn sun. Mrs Wychett was a great walker. She turned and went on again. There was nothing now between her and the skyline, and the sun was warm on her face.

Presently the path dipped, and there was a small, almost circular hollow full of grass. She went down into it, out of sight of everybody in the world now, and sat down. The sun filled the hollow with an almost summer warmth. She sat for a bit with drooping eyelids, and then leant back against the slope and lay full length with her eyes shut. Her body was weighed down with an enormous languor and her mind quick and restless with the lack of the one thing she wanted. She seemed to be waiting, consciously but against all reason, for what she knew could not happen. After a bit, the thing became unbearable, and she sat up sharply. There was still nothing but the green hollow with the sun beating down into it from the misty sky. She got up and went back to the lip behind her. There below her was the school, half hidden under the belt of trees, and beyond it, across the invisible river, the north face of the glen reaching up and away to the distance, where the snow peaks swam in the haze. It was all intolerably peaceful, and suddenly she could not bear the sight of it.

She went hurrying down the track, anxious now to get down under the trees again, and go indoors, and put her town clothes on, and get the car out and go and do her shopping. She got to the house breathless and almost sick with misery. She saw nobody all the way.

XVI

Richard said, 'Manage your shoping all right?'

'Yes, thank you. Except the medicated powder and the mouthwash. I'm keeping them in hand.'

'You weren't summoned?'

'By our Janet? No, thank goodness.'

'I wondered, because I gather she's on the warpath.'

'Where did you get that from?'

'Godwin, when I gave him the photos back. I slipped them to him privily in a corner of the common room, as if I was selling him feelthy peectures on the docks.'

She did not like his simile, but could not say so. She said, 'What did he say?'

'Not much then. Too many people about. But we had a chance to talk later. I gather she knows about the photographs and is asking to see them. He says he's damned if he shows them to her, but he's only stalled so far.'

'Oh dear. I sympathise with him, but I think he's being silly, all the same. I told him this would happen.'

'You knew about it?'

'I knew she knew about the photos, because I told her myself. At least, she apparently guessed in some way, and asked me direct. That was yesterday morning. I told you she'd been bloody. Of course I wasn't going to make a mystery of it. She was obviously disappointed to hear you approved. That's the way her mind works. But I told Peter when he brought the prints, and I warned him she'd be wanting to see them. That's the way her mind works, too. She's determined to be in on anything that's going. He said

148

then he wouldn't let her see them. I couldn't persuade him, of course. He's not open to persuasion. But I still think he's being silly.'

She kept her tone light and conversational, but he was looking at her with a concern that made her ill at ease. He said, 'I told you. The prima donna. I agree with you. Of course the woman's impossible, but we've all got to live with her.'

She was not going to let him off the hook entirely. She said, 'I suppose so.'

He looked for a moment as if he was going to pursue the matter, but he thought better of it. Even so, he left his train of thought visible. He said, 'Haskell's agreed to my having a special history set. I've got four or five boys. They've all got another couple of years here. Two of them aren't much good, but the others have distinct possibilities. It would be nice if we could get one or two university entrances. Hardly scholarships yet, but places at least.'

She said, 'That is good.' She meant it, but her mind was full of a desperate ambivalence, so that she dared not look ahead at all.

He said, 'I've got to go back this evening, I'm afraid. Someone's fallen out, and I've got to take an evening prep. One can't dodge these things altogether. I'll be back for supper, of course.'

Her mind suddenly went very quiet. She said, 'Oh dear.' She said it in a tone of regret that did not amount to any degree of obstruction. Two syllables, and her blackest and most calculated lie yet. 'Oh well,' she said, 'you'll be able to do your own work while you're at it, won't you?'

'Oh yes. It's just that I'll be doing it there instead of here.'

She nodded. 'Supper when, then?' she said.

'Better say eight to be sure. Will that be all right?'

'Of course, yes. I'll have it ready for when you come back.'

She cleared and washed up the tea things, but made no physical move towards getting their supper. Her mind worked furiously, planning in detail what she would do when he left. She prided herself on being a clever cook rather than a very refined or spectacular one, but she had never envisaged clever cookery as an instrument of domestic treachery. Something which looked elaborate, but took no time at all and could be kept hot. She did not let herself look beyond the immediate problem. She had no reason to think anything would come of it, but she planned desperately on the chance. It was nearly five when he left, and getting dark. She saw him off in due form and almost ran to the kitchen. Twice she went to the telephone, but could not bring herself to lift the receiver. Partly it was fear of complications at the other end, but mainly it was an unanswerable instinct to leave the rest to chance. She was not ready yet for concerted intrigue and the planned assignation. There must still be something she had not deliberately brought about.

She got the food in the oven and laid the table. She left the reading lamp on in the sitting-room and a light in the kitchen. It was all as calculated as a stage set. She would be back by a quarter to eight, but if he got home before her, she must be able to say that she had got supper ready and then gone out for a breath of air before they ate it. She did not change her clothes at all. She put on a dark coat over them and dropped a small torch into the pocket. She stood in the hall, looking at the total effect through the open doors of the sitting-room and kitchen. She could not see anything wrong. Then she went out and shut the door quietly behind her.

There was no daylight left now, but the sky was clear and the darkness not absolute. In any case, she dared not use

150

the torch here. She went up the path, moving quicker as her sight improved. The only fixed time was the time she had to be home, but she hurried as if to an appointment. Under the trees it was much darker, but she could still pick her way between the trunks, and when she came to the last of them, the hillside beyond looked luminous and identifiable under the stars. She came out on to the transverse path, and then for the first time stopped, uncertain what to do but still unwilling to admit to herself that she had no plan to work on and nothing to do but wait. She had seen herself going up the track to her green hollow in the hill-face, but common sense told her that if he came, he would almost certainly come along the path. From there he might perhaps go down through the trees towards the house, but he would not go up. She hung there, leaning against the last of the trees, while the urgency and assurance seeped slowly out of her, and she began to feel cold. Both her body and her mind demanded movement, and the only way to move was left-handed along the path, because that was where he would come from, if he came at all. She pulled herself away from the tree and set out along the path.

After a little it started to go downhill. She must be clear of the school buildings by now, and she supposed the path would drop down to the river at some point east of them. That might be where the crossing was, his way of crossing the water other than over the bridge. But it was no use going that far. The only thing to do was to go back to a point above the house and wait there. She was resigned to waiting now. She even saw herself waiting until the time was up, and going back down the hill to give Richard his supper. All the same, she would wait. She turned and went back up the path. She did not know, even afterwards, what had happened or how he had got there, but he was waiting for her just where she had been waiting, in the top edge of the trees.

151

When it came to the point, neither of them said anything at all. She took it for granted that the thing had been as clear in his mind as it had been in hers, and its actual implementation left nothing to be said. Their minds had conceived it directly between them, without the intervention of words, and that made it right and inevitable. The need for words did not come until a little later, when she said, 'Not here, darling. Come on. I know a place.' She took him by the hand and led him up to her green hollow in the hill. She lay down exactly where she had lain that morning, but with the clear stars over her instead of the misted sun, and pulled him down to her. There was a desperate urgency in both of them, and when he came into her, the enormous aching pleasure of her dream surged through her at once, building up like a breaking wave to engulf her waking senses.

Later, with a calm and perfectly cheerful deliberation, she took her arm from his neck and looked at her watch. She said, 'I must go in ten minutes,' and he said, 'All right.' There was too much reassurance in them to argue about the time. They walked down the hill slowly hand in hand. Everything round them seemed as clear as daylight, but she knew that in fact they could not be seen, even if there was anyone to see. When they came to the trees, she said, 'Don't come any farther.'

'You'll be all right?' he said.

'Of course.'

'When shall I see you again?'

'I don't know. Thursday, I suppose. Leave it, anyhow.'

'All right.' They kissed, quite gently, and he went off eastwards along the path and she turned down into the darkness under the trees.

She still had time in hand, and there was no room left in her mind for apprehension. She had drunk the milk of paradise, and nothing could touch her now. She went carefully and quietly over the slippery bed of pine needles, finding her way between the trunks as easily as she had by daylight. She was so sunk in peace that she heard the sound for a moment or two before it established its claim on her conscious attention. Then she stopped and listened.

It came from straight ahead of her, down near the bottom edge of the trees. It was an animal sound, a soft intermittent growling that rose occasionally to a whine. It came from a living throat, but she could not associate it with any creature she knew. It was a nasty little noise, rising and falling down there in the darkness between her and the refuge of her house. The warmth and peace drained out of her, and she felt suddenly frightened. She stood, clutching her coat round her and peering into the trees ahead. She could not see a thing.

It came quite suddenly into an open space hardly ten yards from her. It was silent now. Even its movement over the pine needles made no sound. It came on uncertainly towards her, crouched close to the ground, its pointed head swinging from side to side. It was quite big. Her hand went to her mouth in a childish gesture of terror. She did not scream, but she could not move. Then, as she stared at it, it reared up suddenly and uncertainly on its hind legs and stood there with its front legs dangling in front of it like arms and its head still swinging from side to side. There was no detail in it. All she could see was the dark swaying shape. It looked horribly simian. Then, suddenly and quite distinctly, it said, 'Och, hell!' and dropped on to all fours again. At the same moment a waft of air came uphill to her between the trees, bringing with the sour acid smell of alcohol and vomit.

A surge of relief and disgust swept over her, so sudden and violent that now, when there was no longer anything to be frightened of, she let out a yelp from behind her clenched hand. It was only a small sound, and Alec did not

153

hear it. He was still on his hands and knees, his cap pulled down almost over his eyes, retching repetitively over the clean dry pine needles. She began to move, as quietly as she knew how, going round in a circle between the tree trunks behind him. When she was past him, she went faster, and at the same moment she saw the faint lights of the house down the path ahead. She threw caution to the winds and started to run. She ran wildly, stumbling down the path. She ran round the corner of the house to the door, almost hysterical now with a mixture of laughter and horror, and a moment later Richard had her by the arms. 'What the hell's the matter?' he said.

She clung to him. 'Oh, Richard,' she said. 'It's Alec. He's drunk. He was rolling about on the path. He scared me out of my wits.'

He still held her tight. 'Are you all right?' he said.

'Oh yes, yes. Of course I'm all right. He didn't so much as know I was there.' Even in her distress she had her story ready. 'I just went out for a breath of air before supper,' she said. 'I went up the path, and there he was. I almost stepped on him. It was horrible, in the dark like that. But I'm all right now.'

He said, 'Shall I go up and see to him?'

'Oh no, no. Leave him alone. He'll find his way home eventually. He's being horribly sick. For God's sake come inside and leave him.'

He seemed doubtful. He said, 'What the hell's he doing up here?'

'I don't know. I don't imagine he knows where he is. I've never seen anyone in that state. But he'll get over it. Anyhow, it's no business of ours.'

'All right,' he said. 'We'll give him time to get over it. I'll go up later and if he's still there, I'll phone Macalister.' He opened the door and they went together into the house.

She looked it all over, carefully and critically, as she had before she went out. It still looked all right. She took her coat off, and there she was in her ordinary indoor clothes, just as she had come out of the kitchen. Her shoes were damp on her feet, but this did not show. 'You go on in,' she said. 'I'll just straighten up. I'm sorry I got in such a state, but it really was a bit nasty. Supper's all ready. I'll be with you in a moment.'

He took his books and papers into the sitting-room and she hung her coat up. The back of it was damp from the dew on the grass, but this, too, you could not tell by looking at it. She looked herself over in the glass. Before, in the days of her physical innocence, she found her face full of guilt, but now it looked as it had always looked. The recent, ridiculous disturbance steamed off from the top of her mind, and the almost physical glow came back. She felt warm and secure and very cunning. She washed her hands and straightened her hair and went through into the kitchen. The food, when she took it out of the oven, was perfect too. It was all ridiculously easy when you set your mind to it, and now even the nagging restlessness had gone out of her. There was nothing more she wanted, and she was content to do the honours of her home.

The meal was a success. When they had finished, Richard said, 'What about that chap? Shall I go up and see? Perhaps I'd better.'

'If you like,' she said. 'So long as you don't expect me to come with you. Only take a torch and don't step in the mess. My shoes seem to be all right. We don't want it on yours.'

'I'll go carefully,' he said. 'Where was he, exactly?'

'Just straight up the hill, in the edge of the trees. If he's still there, you'll see him all right. But I don't think he will be. He's probably used to it.'

He took the torch and went out, and she set about clearing the supper. He was not gone long. She heard him come in and put the torch down in the hall. 'No sign of him,' he said when he came in. 'But you're right about the mess. The place reeks. We need rain. I still wonder where the hell he'd been, to be up there in that state.'

She said, 'He probably won't remember, anyway,' but she herself knew. It had come to her suddenly, and she did not much like it. She remembered what Peter had said about Alec. 'Of course you could make him drunk.' A task for heroes or millionaires, he had called it. She wondered how much Peter was prepared to invest in the extraction of information from that dark, animal silence, and what dividends he had had from his investment. Whatever it was, she did not think Peter would have got drunk himself. She could not imagine him drunk in any circumstances. His hard, amused mind would have sat back from the uncouth conviviality, stirring the pot and waiting to see what took shape in it.

Richard said, 'I suppose not. All the same, I think I'll have a word with Macalister when I see him. We don't want him coming up here.'

She thought about this. She could see no harm in it, and in any case could say nothing against it. 'If you like,' she said. 'But he's probably used to his Alec's goings-on by now. He was perfectly harmless, in fact. Just rather nasty.'

He nodded, but did not commit himself. 'I dare say,' he said.

She finished the washing up and went and joined him in the sitting-room. He had got through his work at the school, and now he was reading the paper, but without much concentration. They sat there, placid and well fed and rather drowsy, and she was gradually aware that when they went to bed, he would want to make love to her. She always knew. For all their reticence, in this matter at least their minds and bodies had so grown together that no overt communication was necessary. But she could not have it tonight. It was a thing she would have to come to terms with, but she must have time. After a bit she said. 'I'm very tired, Richard. I suppose it was getting into a fright over Alec. I think I'll go to bed.'

He looked at her. This was an agreed signal, but he did not want to accept it, or perhaps he wanted to know the reason for it. He looked at her long and appraisingly, but their rules allowed no question and no argument. 'All right,' he said. 'I'm sorry. You go on, then.'

He turned back to his paper, and she got up and left him. The vast contentment still held her, but under it she was conscious of a small, fresh niggle of worry. While she got ready for bed, she wondered what Peter had been up to.

XVII

There was no summons this time, and not even any warning. The bell rang sharply, and when she opened the door, Janet Haskell stepped forward at once, as if she was afraid of having the door shut in her face. It was a face to shut the door on, unbecomingly flushed, with the eyes hard and wide open. She said, 'Mrs Wychett, I must see you. May I come in and speak to you for a moment?'

This was not the woman who had wanted to use Christian names. It was not even a woman you would think of offering coffee to. You could not, by the rules, keep her out, but you dealt with her as if she was a debt-collector. She did not seem to expect anything else. Kate could not see what she herself had done to warrant this, not if you played by the rules, but then half the time Janet Haskell did not. For a single appalling moment she connected the change with what had happened up on the hill last night, but she did not really believe that even Janet Haskell could know about that. She looked at her equally hard and direct, but conscious of an enormous shrinking inside herself. Whatever it was she had to deal with, it frightened and sickened her. 'Oh?' she said. 'Of course. Come in.'

She did not suggest that Mrs Haskell should take her coat off, nor did she make any move to. It was dry, and any irrelevant action was not to be considered. She turned and led the way into the sitting-room, and Mrs Haskell shut the front door behind her and followed her in. When they got there, Kate turned and faced her. She did not ask her to sit down either. She just stood there, waiting for her to speak.

She did not seem to find this easy. She had probably

worked herself up into a state of fury at home, after her husband had gone over to the school, and had come hurrying up here on the impulse, because there was nowhere else she could go. Now that she was here, even she was conscious of the unreasonableness of what she was doing and was at a loss how to begin. Kate said, 'Mrs Haskell, are you sure it's me you want to talk to?'

She knew she had scored a hit, but she also knew that she would have done better not to. So long as the social pretences were maintained, she could use her superior expertise to advantage. Once they were down, its mere existence was an offence. They were down now. Mrs Haskell, as she had thought, was in a fury, and the suggestion that she was being unreasonable only made it worse. She said, 'And why should I not speak to you? You're all in this together, are you not?'

Kate surprised even herself by the strength and suddenness of her sense of relief. Whatever it was, this could be nothing to do with James, or not directly. Not even Mrs Haskell could believe in any general conspiracy there. It must still be the photographs, and here she was on infinitely firmer ground. Her confidence counselled gentleness. She did not think she could ever again feel sorry for Mrs Haskell, but at least she had no wish to make things worse for her. All she wanted now was to soothe her as far as she could be soothed, and then get rid of her. To get rid of her was the paramount need. She said, 'I don't know what it is worrying you, but do please believe me, I'm not in anything, not with other people, not against you.' As a statement it lacked precision, but it was a denial in the terms of the charge, and she thought Mrs Haskell would understand it. She did. She said, 'Have you not been talking to Mr Godwin, then?'

It was the photographs, all right. She took up with thankfulness a posture of innocence and sweet reason. She

said, 'Mr Godwin? Not since —' She hesitated for a moment, and this time there was no calculation in it. She
looked back across a gulf of time to a different world. But it
was only two days. 'Not since the day before yesterday,' she
said. She thought for a moment, and then moved straight
on into what she took to be the enemy's country. 'He
brought the photographs down for us to see,' she said. It
was all calculation now. She gave Mrs Haskell a small
deprecating smile. 'The ones he had taken of me, you know.
Richard and I picked the one we liked, and he gave them
back to him next day, I think.'

Mrs Haskell was still glaring at her. Her smile had
melted on that burning stare. She looked very big like that,
standing up in the middle of the sitting-room with her
heavy coat belted round her. She was a big woman, and a
strong one. Kate wondered suddenly what she would do if
Mrs Haskell actually went for her. She did not know what
she could do. She had never been physically afraid of a
woman before. Her social defences would be useless against
physical violence. She felt like a lion-tamer who suddenly
finds his authority gone, and has to fall back on the primeval superiority of human cunning. Her relative innocence
was no good now. She must lie and lie again if necessary,
anything to pacify this big fierce woman and get her out of
the house before she lost the last of her self-control. Mrs
Haskell said, 'That was after I had spoken to you about
them?'

The question was no more than a shade of intonation.
The words were a statement of historical fact, which both
knew to be true. Kate put up a pretence of momentary
thought. 'Yes,' she said. 'Yes, that's right.'

Mrs Haskell smiled now, only with her mouth, but she
did smile. She was like a brow-beating cross-examiner who
has got the answer he wanted out of a reluctant witness, and
smiles down at his papers. She said, 'And did you not tell

Mr Godwin of our conversation?'

Kate herself was angry now. She had let herself be forced into a lie on a matter in which she herself had no reason to lie at all. But she knew she had no alternative. She stared back at Mrs Haskell, a cold stare against her hot one. 'No,' she said. 'No, I didn't. Why should I?'

Mrs Haskell smiled again. When she stopped pretending, she was much more formidable, even mentally, than Kate had thought possible. She said, 'Did you not think it would be of interest to him?'

Kate said, 'The thing just didn't arise. Mr Godwin brought the photos for me to see, and we discussed them, and then he left them here and went.'

'For you to see? Was your husband not here?'

'Not when Mr Godwin first came. He came home a little later, when Mr Godwin was still here. Then we all looked at them, and then Mr Godwin left. And then, as I say, Richard gave them back to him next day.'

Mrs Haskell nodded. 'Then why will he not show them to me?' she said.

Kate said, 'I can't think why. Have you asked him?'

Mrs Haskell nodded again but said nothing. 'Well,' said Kate, 'that's for Mr Godwin to say, not me. If I had them here, you could see them with pleasure. That's if they're really of any interest to you. I can't think why they should be. But they're not here, I'm afraid. I think Richard has asked Mr Godwin for a print or two of the one we like, and when we have it, you can see that, if you really want to. But for the moment I can't help you.'

For quite a long time Mrs Haskell still said nothing. They still looked at each other. Mrs Haskell did not believe her. She would almost certainly not have believed her even if what she had said was true, but it was not true. Even in this wholly ridiculous business of the photographs she had put herself in the wrong, and she did not like the feeling.

You talked about people to other people, and sometimes you lied to people direct, but always on the assumption that you would never be directly challenged on what you had said. You made that assumption because people behaved in a particular way, and the direct challenge was not within the rules. When somebody suddenly broke the rules and challenged you, you found yourself at a loss. You could be indignant with them for breaking the rules, but your indignation did not, when it came to the point, altogether get you over the fact that you could not meet their challenge. She remembered her sudden spurt of anger when James had said she was not being fair to him. Now Mrs Haskell was not being fair to her. She was behaving ridiculously and impossibly, but she had, for the moment, a sort of uncouth moral advantage At last she took her eyes off Kate. She lifted one of her large capable hands and looked at it, as if considering its strength. She said, 'You're a lying woman, Mrs Wychett.'

She said it quite quietly, and the appalling thing about it was that it was true. So far as Mrs Haskell was directly concerned, there was only this business of the photographs, where she had been cornered and had lied almost against her will. But there was the much larger and more deadly lie of her affair with James, and that, with or without reason, undermined her whole position. She could no longer say to hell with them, let them say what they liked. The thing had happened now. She could still outface them, but not it. She hated Mrs Haskell from the bottom of her heart, but she could not take up her challenge. All she wanted now was to get rid of her. She said, equally quietly, 'Don't you think you had better go now, Mrs Haskell?'

'Oh ay,' said Mrs Haskell. I'm going, right enough.' She had abandoned the headmaster's wife completely. She was just Janet Cameron, the daughter of the widow Cameron from along the glen. It did not maker her any easier to deal with. She was looking at Kate again now. 'But I'm warning you, Mrs Wychett,' she said, 'you're making trouble here, and it's yourself mostly you're making trouble for.' She looked away again, and spoke with a sudden harsh vehemence, as if she was making a general pronouncement and not merely speaking for Kate's benefit. 'That James Macalister,' she said, 'he was never any good to any woman.' She looked at Kate again. 'You'll be finding that out for yourself directly, unless I'm much mistaken.'

Kate's control snapped suddenly, and her fear went with it. All she wanted now was to hurt. 'Damn you,' she said, 'damn you for a bitter, jealous woman. What I think of Mr Macalister is my concern, but by God, I know what you feel about him. If he crooked his little finger, you'd go running to him tomorrow, headmaster's wife or no headmaster's wife. It's not me that's making trouble here. There was plenty of trouble already before I came, and I know who's at the bottom of most of it. Now get out, or I'll telephone the school and ask your husband to come and take you away.'

For a moment she thought Mrs Haskell really was going to attack her, and in her fury she almost hoped she would. The two women faced each other in that quiet, elegant room, fists clenched, eyes staring, full of a greater mutual hatred than any two men could manage, but lacking the man's natural outlet in senseless physical violence. Then, all at once, Mrs Haskell broke down. It was very sudden and very horrifying. The last time she had hidden her face before Kate had known what was happening, and Kate had never been sure, even at the end, whether her distress had been genuine. But now she still stood there, facing her, as her great flushed face crumpled and puckered, and the hard mouth gaped a little, and the staring eyes half closed as two big single tears rolled out of them and ran slowly down into the gaping mouth. She was grotesque in her grief as she had never been in her anger, and Kate, watching her, felt only revulsion and still no pity.

Very slowly Mrs Haskell turned her back on her. She did not put her hands to her face, or even follow the ordinary woman's instinct to grope for a handkerchief and mop up as best she could the mess she had made of her face. She just stood there, with her hands clenching and un-clenching at her sides. She made no sound at all. Kate thought she would go now. Surely she must go. There was surely nothing more to be said that either of them could bear to hear said. Silence was the only thing left. She could not even make a move herself. There could be no shepherd-ing her to the door this time, because no social restraints any longer applied. She could only stand there, as long as she could endure it, and wait.

Mrs Haskell did not go. To Kate's almost incredulous horror, she turned slowly and faced her again. Her eyes were closed almost to slits, so that the whole face looked like a mask, one of those stylised, grotesque masks of primi-tive drama or the devil dance. And like a mask, the face no longer cried, though the mouth still gaped a little, as if to allow a human voice to speak from behind it. She said, 'I could have had him. I could have had him on your terms,' and that was true, too.

Kate said, 'Go. For God's sake, go.' She said it almost in a whisper, and her hands came up in front of her in a defensive gesture, though it was no longer physical violence she was frightened of.

In some horrifying way, Mrs Haskell was more in control of the situation than she was. Perhaps she had long since come to terms with herself, secretly, in a way Kate had not, but whatever it was, she knew what she was doing now more than Kate did. She said, 'Ay, I'd best be going. It's no place for me here.' She said it with a sort of deep inward disgust, so that Kate suddenly saw, for the first time, that the revulsion she herself felt was mutual. She was as horrifying to the other woman as the other woman was to her. It had never occurred to her that she could be, and it seemed the worst single thing that had happened since Mrs Haskell had appeared at the door. She said nothing. She had nothing to say. She just stood there, waiting for her to go.

She went, in the end, quite quickly and quietly. Her eyes opened a little, and she gave Kate a long look. She seemed to be concentrating, thinking hard, but you could not tell at all what she was thinking about. Then she turned and walked out. She walked out into the hall, and Kate let her go. She did not move until she heard the front door open and shut. Then she went into the kitchen, and drew a glass of water from the tap and rinsed her mouth out. She did not drink any of the water, but ran it through her mouth and spat it out into the sink. She could not have said why she did it, but it was what she needed to do. Then she went back into the sitting-room.

There was nothing she could do at all. That was the first fact she had to come to terms with. There was nothing she could do and no one she could talk to. The thing was between her and Mrs Haskell. As for James, James was the last person she could talk to about it. James was what it was all about, but she could not talk to him about it. She wondered about Peter Godwin. She even longed to tell him about it, but she did not blink the light that this threw on her own desolation. Peter was an inhuman creature, subject to no ordinary feelings or constraints. He had taken a blackmailing photograph of her for his own amusement, but had no wish even to blackmail her with it. Peter was her only possible confidant.

Perhaps there was, after all, one thing she could do. Perhaps she could get away from the place altogether. She could offer some explanation, any explanation other than

165

the truth, and leave Richard here, where he was beginning to enjoy himself, and go south on her own. But she was not sure she could make herself go, not yet, and in any case she was afraid of explanations with Richard, even explanations of her wanting to go. Things were no worse than they had been before Mrs Haskell's visit, no worse and no better. She had always known Mrs Haskell hated her, and she had always known why, and whatever new truths she had discovered in herself, she had given nothing away to the enemy. Mrs Haskell, like the rest of the glen, worked on the worst available assumptions, but she had acquired no new facts. She was dangerous, frighteningly dangerous, but no more than she had been that first evening when Richard, rather than Kate herself, had seen the danger in her. There was still a decision to be made, but it did not rest with Mrs Haskell.

It was fine and bright outside. The clear night had brought a clear day. She thought she would walk, not over the bridge where Mrs Haskell could see her, and not right up the near hill-face, where all the world could see her if they chose to look, but eastward along the path at the top of the trees. No one would be on the path at this time of the morning. In the dusk it would be different. In the dusk James would be up there waiting, and she knew that if Richard was not at home, she would go up to him. She also knew that she hoped Richard would be at home. She could not talk to anyone, but for one day at least she wanted the decision out of her hands.

XVIII

For more than twenty-four hours she saw no one but Richard. They were perfectly friendly and polite. She could not get over the feeling that he was in some way no longer immediately involved. All the time the weather was clear and still, with the same misted sun by day and the same clear stars at night. All the time the tension built up inside her, but she did not know what she could do. She was obsessed with the fear that in some way things were being decided for her over her head, but she did not know how or by whom.

When Peter Godwin came, she welcomed him with a relief she made no attempt to hide. He came in the afternoon, earlier than he had come before, and he brought the photographs in an envelope in his hand. She said, 'Oh, Peter, come in. I'm glad to see you.'

He looked at her with the same bright, speculative excitement she had seen in him before, but his manner was gentle enough. 'Are you?' he said. 'I ought to be pleased. Well, I am, in a way. But I hope it doesn't mean trouble. Trouble for you, I mean. I don't really expect it to be just for my bright eyes.'

She shook her head, but said nothing. When it came to the point, she did not really know what it was she wanted to tell him. 'Well, anyhow,' he said, 'here are the finished prints.' He gave her the envelope, and she pulled the photographs out. There were two copies of the portrait of a lady. She was no longer really interested in it, but was still moved to admiration by its sheer quality. *Such an one I was this present. Is't not well done?* She knew it was herself, but it

167

was not the self she was immediately aware of. There was a third print underneath. Before she uncovered it, she looked at Peter. His eyes were still excited about something, but there was no threat in them. She looked down again and pulled the photograph out from under the others. It was Catriona, beautifully, even lovingly, finished. The background was almost faded out, and there was just the face, full of its secret radiance, so that it almost broke her heart to look at it.

'Oh, Peter,' she said, 'it's lovely.'

He smiled at her, a little shamefaced, as if he surprised himself by the pleasure he got from hers. 'I thought you might have a use for it,' he said. 'Only – well, look, Richard didn't ask for it, so I'd rather he didn't see it. Do you mind?'

She did not want to answer him directly. She shook her head again. 'I'll put it away,' she said. She put the two official portraits back into the envelope and put the envelope on the table. 'Don't go,' she said. 'I won't be a moment.' She took the third photograph through into her bedroom and stored it among her things in a place where she knew it would not be disturbed. When she came back, Peter was sitting there, looking at her.

'Now, what's the trouble?' he said.

'Mrs Haskell, of course,' she said. 'I had her here again yesterday. Peter, she frightens me to death, she hates me so. And what you said about her – do you remember? – it's true, I'm afraid.'

He nodded. 'Straight sex?' he said.

'Yes.'

He frowned, looking at the floor. Then he said, 'All right, I'm going to tell you the whole story. I think I'd better. I know it now.'

'Alec?'

'Yes. How did you know?'

168

'I saw him, the other evening. He was so drunk he couldn't stand. I guessed what you'd been up to. I didn't know what results you'd got, of course.'

'You needn't sound so contemptuous,' he said. 'I'm not in the least repentant. In a place like this the truth is the only thing worth having. It's hard enough to come by, God knows, but without it you can't cope with all the lies. Not really, I mean. You can ignore them, or try to, but they still bite a little. You know that.'

'Yes,' she said, 'all right. I wasn't really contemptuous. It just seemed a little cold-blooded.'

'So it was. I don't go in for hot blood much, myself. There's too much of it here without my adding to it.'

She said, 'Go on.'

'Well – it's simple, really. Hackneyed, almost. Mrs Cameron, Janet Haskell's mother, was an old love-light of the laird's. The old laird, I mean. He took up with her after his wife died. She wasn't here then. This was over to the east somewhere. She moved here later, and he put her in the cottage along the glen. I think the thing was over by then, but she had a hold on him, of course. She had a daughter. His daughter. Janet and James are brother and sister. Half-brother and half-sister, anyhow.'

'But —'

'James didn't know, of course. No one knew except the old man and Mrs Cameron. And what the old man knew, Alec knew. He wouldn't marry Mrs Cameron, but I fancy she made him pay out. And of course, she wouldn't let him sell out to Cotton's. He was broke to the wide, and it was about his only hope, but she wouldn't have it. By all accounts, a bitch if ever there was one. Our Janet's got bad blood in her, all right.'

'Then what happened?'

'Well, that was the situation. I don't know how long it would have lasted or what would have happened in the end.

169

But then Janet came on the scene. A big juicy Janet, hell-bent on bettering herself. And there was James, bored and restless and at loggerheads with the old man. Of course he started making passes at her, and she played him along, and the old man found out. I don't suppose for a moment that James meant to marry her, but there are things one would rather didn't happen, even short of marriage. So the old man told James the facts. That really tore it. There was a final flaming row, and James got out. Janet consoled herself with John Haskell. She didn't know, of course. She still doesn't, obviously. Then the old laird had his accident. I think Alec knows what really happened, but he wouldn't come clean on that, drunk or sober. My own guess is that the old man couldn't go on, and took his own way out. Any-way, that brought James back, and he sold at once. He could afford to, do you see? For one thing, the widow Cameron had nothing on him. His father had been the grand old man of the glen, but James couldn't care less what happened to his dad's reputation. And there was another thing, much more important. Janet was the headmaster's wife now. She had done very well for herself. Whatever she felt, the old bitch wasn't likely to want it put about that her up-stage daughter was the old laird's bastard. So she had no defence against James, and out she went, and in came Cotton's, and there was James, sitting fairly pretty. But – well, you see, he knows who Janet Haskell is. So whatever she feels about him, he's safe enough about her. I thought there'd be no harm in your knowing that.'

Kate said, 'The picture, of course. I knew there was something.'

'What picture?'

'The old laird. At the lodge. You haven't seen it? It's not a bit like James, but I felt there was something familiar. The eys, I think. Not a nice face. If the mother was bad too, no wonder she's what she is.' She was not thinking of James at all. Her mind ran wholly on Janet Haskell. For all Peter's assurances, the thing frightened her more than ever. She said, 'Peter, she must never know. Whatever happens, she must never know. She's only barely sane as it is. If she found this out, I think she'd crack altogether. There's no saying what she might do. Can't you see that?'

He thought about this. 'I can see two things,' he said. 'First, there'd be pure jealousy and resentment. The hatred of the bastard for the legitimate heir. It's in all the plays. If the old man had done right by her mother, she'd have been brought up at the lodge along with James. She'd have been gentry. That would mean a hell of a lot to her. That would be one thing. And then of course there's the sex thing. She still hankers after James, and this puts him out of reach finally.'

Kate said, 'It's not as simple as that. She has this tremendous – I don't know, respectability, priggishness almost. It's not all social ambition. Don't you know what I mean?'

'I do know, yes. I'd say the old woman tried to purge her own indiscretions by giving her daughter a hell-fire upbringing. And that, sitting on top of the raw Janet, probably plays hell with her. And being married to poor old Haskell won't help.'

'Yes, but you see, she'd be horrified – horrified at what she might have done, horrified at what she still wants to do. It wouldn't be logical, but she'd feel branded, in a way you and I couldn't in a hundred years. I tell you, she might do anything.'

He said, 'Well, she won't find out from me. Or, I imagine, from you. And there's no reason why James should tell her. I don't know about the mother. I don't even know if she's still alive. But if she's kept quiet all this time, I assume she'll go on keeping quiet. I'm not sure you're right about the effect it might have if she did find out. I think in some ways it might settle her mind for her a bit. But in any case, I don't see any reason why she ever should.' He thought for a moment. 'One thing,' he said. 'I've told you this in confidence, because I got it out of Alec. If James chooses to tell you at some point, that's his affair, but you mustn't let him know you know, because that would make trouble for Alec. Is that all right?'

'Yes,' said Kate, 'yes. I've no wish to tell anyone. I'm glad you told me, I think. As you say, the truth is the only defence here. So thank you, Peter. But please let's not have it mentioned again, ever. It's an old wrong, and better buried. Wrongs live too long in the Highlands, anyway. For God's sake let's do nothing to dig it up.' She looked at him. If he was not kind, at least he was uncensorious and not unsympathetic. 'Oh, Peter,' she said, 'I'm frightened. I can't see any good end to anything. What am I to do?'

He said, 'Richard's the real trouble, isn't he?'

'Richard?'

'He's settling in. He's loving it. For what that's worth, he's doing the school all the good in the world. You can't shift him now, can you?'

She shook her head. 'No', she said. 'No, you're quite right. That is the trouble, really.'

'Then go without him. He may or may not know why you're going, but he won't stop you. It needn't be permanent. But get away now, and at least give things a chance to settle down a bit. Can't you?'

She felt swamped by an appalling sense of desolation, but there was still only one thing she could do. 'I'll try,' she said.

'Try,' he said. 'I like you very much, Kate. I always have, right from the start. But I want you out of here. For everyone's sake. Mostly your own.' Then he got up and went. The envelope with its two elegant photographs still lay on the table. She did not want even to touch it.

Richard came back in a sort of detached good humour. He did not talk about the school, but she had the feeling that in his mind he had not completely left it. He looked at the photographs with critical approval, as if they were a set of new curtains for the sitting-room. She knew what she had to say to him, and she did not doubt, now, her ability to say it. It was just a matter of choosing the moment.

It came between tea and supper. There was suddenly nothing to prevent her saying what she had to say, and she dared not put it off. She said, 'Richard,' and then stopped, to make sure she had his attention. He lifted his eyes from what he was doing and looked at her. She had a sudden, disconcerting feeling that he knew what she was going to say and had been expecting her to say it before. She said, 'Do you think you could manage here on your own if I went south for a bit?'

He answered quietly and at once. He said, 'Yes, if that's what you want.'

'It's what I need. I don't think it need be for long. But I don't want to disturb you. Above all, I don't want that, and I'm not sure how you're going to manage, working the hours you do.'

He said, 'I might move in with Peter Godwin. He's said to be a good housekeeper, and his hours are easier than mine. I'm about the one member of the staff who could do it without anyone's bothering to lift an eyebrow, and for that very reason I think he might agree. We'd get on all right.' He had thought it all out. She knew that with absolute certainty. She even wondered for a moment whether he had envisaged the arrangement as permanent. He did not ask her why she wanted to go. She supposed he knew that, too, or some of it. Please God, only some of it. He said, 'Where will you go?'

'I thought Geraldine's. She's got room, and I think she'd be glad to have me for a bit.'

If he found the innocence of the situation reassuring, he did not show it. He said, 'Yes, that's a good idea. She certainly wouldn't be one for the Highlands herself, and she'd understand your wanting to get away for a bit. When will you go?'

'Well – as soon as you can make your arrangements, I think.'

He nodded. 'I'll speak to Peter,' he said. And that was all.

The implications of what she had done, now that she had done it, grew on her all the evening. She had in some way cleared her conscience, and that gave her the right to be miserable. The misery grew until it threatened to engulf her altogether, and the evening passed on a knife-edge of mutual restraint. At bed time she suddenly found herself wanting Richard to make love to her, just for the comfort of his bed, but he made no move at all. She lay there, flat and rigid in the darkness, until she was certain he was asleep. Then she started to cry, hopelessly and as quietly as she could. They talked of crying yourself to sleep, but she wondered if anyone ever really did. Children, perhaps. After a bit she stopped crying and dried her face for the last time so as not to stain the pillow. Then she turned over and settled herself to sleep.

She dreamed that she was up on the hill again, but this time she was consciously looking for James, and could not find him. She knew she had to find him before it was too late, or she would have to go away and not see him again. She never did find him. She called, 'James! James!' but there was no answer, and then she found herself awake. It was getting light. She wondered in a moment of panic

174

whether she had called out audibly in her sleep, but Richard was sleeping sound in the next bed. It was still much too early to get up and make the tea, and she lay there, waiting for the day to start.

XIX

It was one of those dark days, when the clouds hung over the glen, never quite raining, but never seeming to move. The bright weather was over, but then in a day or two she would be in London, where the weather did not matter. When Richard had gone down to the school, she set herself to the problem of packing, what to take and what not to take, how completely to move herself into Geraldine's flat. She had phoned a telegram after breakfast. Geraldine would not mind that, and if she had heard nothing by this evening, she could assume that she was expected. All this was in the front of her mind. The back of her mind was entirely occupied with James. She did not think she could bear either to see him before she left or to go without seeing him. He had once said, almost to himself, that if she left the glen he would follow her, but that would be worse than anything. The telephone was there in the hall, but her old fear of it kept her away from it. If it rang, she knew she would answer it, but she hoped it would not. At some point she remembered the Grants' dinner party, but that was not for another three days. She would leave Richard to deal with that after she had gone. He would have his explanation ready. Probably he already had, even before she had talked of going.

It was well into the afternoon, and already turning towards dusk, when she heard the front door flung open and the sound of hurried feet in the hall. Peter called, 'Kate! Kate! Where are you?' His voice sounded harsh and urgent, and panic gripped her hard in the pit of her stomach. She opened the door of the bedroom and faced him through the doorway. His face was white and hard. There was no amusement left in it.

She said, 'Peter, what's the matter?' and he stood there, looking at her, as if for once he was at a loss for words.

When he did speak, it was as if he was forcing the words out of himself. He said, 'I've just got in. Someone's been at my things. It's been straightened up, more or less, but you can tell.'

He stopped, still looking at her. She asked, because someone had to say something, but she knew already. She said, 'Is anything missing?' and he nodded.

He said, 'She must have come looking for the photographs. She's only taken the one.'

She did not ask which, because there was no need to. He said, 'Kate, what shall I do?'

Her mind was working with a cold desperate clarity. She said, 'Nothing. Don't do anything. Only burn that damned negative.'

'I have. I already had. It was just the one print with the others. I was going to burn that, but I hadn't. How the hell could I expect this? What do you think she'll do?'

Kate said, 'I know what she'll do. Go, Peter, please. Go at once. And don't do anything.'

He hesitated. He said, 'If there's anything —' but she stopped him.

'Only go away,' she said. 'Please, Peter. At once.'

He looked at her for a moment. Then he turned and went. As soon as the door was shut on him, she ran to the phone.

The bell rang for some time at the other end before anyone answered. It was a woman's voice, local, but overlaid with the careful neutrality of the superior servant. It said, 'No, madam, Mr Macalister is not in yet.'

Kate said, 'When do you expect him?'

The voice hesitated. It said, 'Well, I said, not till dinner-

177

time, madam.' It hesitated again, and then said, 'That is Mrs Haskell?'

Kate said, 'No, it's not Mrs Haskell.'

The voice was all apology, but there was, to her ear, a hint of amusement in it, almost of malice. It said, 'Oh, I beg your pardon, madam. I had Mrs Haskell asking for him, and I thought —'

Kate said, 'Can you tell me where Mr Macalister is?' She wanted to ask how long it was since Mrs Haskell had asked the same question, but she dared not.

The voice said, 'He's away up the Corrie Dorcha, madam, after the foxes. We expect him back to dinner.'

Kate said, 'Oh, I see, yes. Very well. Thank you. I'll ring again later.' She put the receiver down before the voice could reply, and went straight out of the house. They did not hunt foxes in this part of the world, they shot them as vermin. She knew that. But surely he would have Alec with him. That was the one hope her mind fastened on, but it was another of the things she could not ask. She walked out through the school buildings and over the bridge. Mrs Wychett going for a walk in the grey of the afternoon, but now there would be no one watching for her. As soon as she was out of sight of the school, she started to run, but she knew she could not keep this up, and after a little she dropped to a walk again, but still going as fast as she could drive herself. She saw no one anywhere. The whole world was grey and empty and completely silent.

When she turned up the path, the corrie hung over her like a long dark funnel, reaching up to the clouds. The clouds were clear of the tops. There was no mist, as there had been in her dream, only a clear waste of dark daylight. She stumbled on a loose stone, which went clattering away among the rocks, and when she recovered herself, she wondered if she had heard a shot up there ahead of her. If it had been a shot, it was muffled by the curve of the hill and she could not be certain. In any case, that was what he was up there for, to shoot a fox. Her physical distress had begun to damp the desperate apprehension of her mind. All she could do was go on, driving herself up the winding, undulating path.

It was the rise and fall of the path that saved her, that and her sheer exhaustion. Near the top of a rise she stopped, doubling herself over to ease the stitch in her side, and in the silence she heard someone running on the path ahead. Whoever it was, she knew with an absolute certainty that it was not James. The running feet had nothing of James in them. She did not even straighten herself. She turned and ran, crouching as she was, into the heather at the side of the path and flung herself flat behind a rock.

She knew who it would be before she saw her, but even so she was not ready for what she saw. Janet Haskell went down the path, within a few yards of her, running as if she would never stop. Her mouth gaped a little and her eyes stared at something she did not see, but she made no sound except the hiss of her labouring breath. Kate stayed there, crouching on her hands and knees like a beast in the heather, until the enemy had gone over the shoulder of the hill. Then she picked herself up and went back to the path. She did not hurry now. She went almost cautiously, stalking in the grey dusk whatever it was she had to find.

She came on him quite suddenly. He was sitting at the top of the slope above the burn. There was a rock at his back, and his shotgun was by his side. He sat with his knees drawn up and one hand hugging his waist. The other hand hung out over his knees with the first clenched tight. She called, 'James!' and he turned his head and looked at her. His mouth was tight shut, but his eyes smiled.

He said, 'Catriona. Did you see her?'

She flung herself down on her knees in front of him. She said, 'Yes, but she didn't see me. James, what happened?

179

Are you all right?'

He looked at her with a sort of mild serenity. He spoke very quietly. 'I'll tell you,' he said. He seemed to be thinking. Then he said, 'She came up after me. I heard her calling. She showed me a photograph. Where did she get it, Catriona?'

'She stole it. From Peter Godwin.'

He nodded. 'Did you know?'

'I knew he had it, yes. Then he told me it had gone, and I found out where you were and came up after you.'

He nodded again. He seemed curiously placid, as if he merely wanted to get the facts straight. He said, 'She showed it to me. She said —' He hesitated, as if he could not find the words for what he had to say. He said, 'She wanted —'

Kate said, 'I know what she wanted, James.'

He looked at her almost apologetically. 'You do?' he said. 'I'm sorry.'

'Never mind. James, what happened?'

'I told her – I told her why it couldn't be done. There were things she didn't know and I had to tell her. Then she – well, she lost control altogether. I don't think she's quite sane, Catriona. I hadn't realised. I suppose I should have known. Anyway, she turned on you then. She told me what she would do, and I couldn't have that, so I went for her. To get the photograph, you see? She fought for it. She was as strong as I was. I hadn't thought she was so strong. And then of course the damned gun went off and I got hit.'

She put her hands on his shoulders, pleading with him for reassurance. She said, 'James, are you all right?'

'I don't know,' he said. He seemed genuinely doubtful. 'I expect so.'

'James, what shall I do?'

He was quite calm and decided now, as if he had the

situation fully under control. He said, 'I want you to go down as fast as you can and telephone the lodge. Tell them where I am and say I've had an accident. They'll know what to do. Will you do that?'

She said, 'Was it an accident? I saw her, James. Why did she have to run like that?'

He gave her a small smile, but again only with his eyes. 'Oh yes,' he said, 'it was an accident. We have accidents in our family. You know that.'

There was nothing more she could say. 'I'll go, then,' she said. 'Will you be all right?'

'I expect so. Anyway, you go on down, will you? As quick as you can.'

'I will,' she said. She stooped over him and put her mouth lightly to his, but his face seemed to go away backwards from under hers. She pulled back and looked at him, and as she looked, his mouth opened a little and a trickle of blood came out of one corner and ran down his chin, dripping over the front of his jacket. Then the mouth shut again, and a bubble formed between his lips and hung there, like a bubble of dark red molten glass. It burst, and another took its place. There were four bubbles altogether, one after the other. Then there was nothing more at all. His eyes still kept their mild blue gaze in her direction, but they did not see her.

She picked herself up slowly and cautiously, like a woman leaving a sleeping husband she does not want to disturb. As she drew back from him, his clenched fist opened, and a tight ball of crumpled paper fell out and rolled down the slope. It stopped between her feet. She stooped and picked it up. She did not look at it at all. She knew what it was.

It was the eyes that held her. She could not leave them like that. She could not bear their uncomprehending benevolence. You closed the eyes of the dead. That was one of

181

the things you did for them. She knew that, but she had never thought how you actually set about it. She managed it at last. It was not difficult when you made up your mind to what you had to do. Then she went off, quite slowly, down the path.

She went twenty yards or so, and then turned off into the heather. She drove her heel repeatedly into the black glutinous soil and dropped the crumpled ball into the bottom of the hole. She covered it over carefully and put dry stuff on the top. When she was back on the path, she even turned to see if she had left any footprints, but she could not see any. Then she went on again, still quite slowly. There was no need to hurry now. There was nothing more she could do for him now. They knew where he was.

XX

The train came in reluctantly, as if it could hardly bring itself to stop for Glenaidon and its single passenger. There were three coaches, two of them sleepers. She supposed it would grow on its way south, just as it had shrunk coming up. She picked up her dressing case and Richard the other two cases. She was travelling first-class, so as to be sure of being alone. That had been Richard's doing. A wife hurrying to join her husband travelled second. A wife being laid off, even temporarily, travelled first. There must be a moral in it somewhere.

The attendant was ready on the step to receive her. She thought he was the small dark Londoner she had had for the first part of her journey up. He looked at the list in his hand and said, 'Mrs Wychett?' He was a southerner, all right. Even in two words you could tell. It was the way he asked the question, as if he really wanted to know, not as if he was telling you. Her heart warmed to him. She said, 'That's right.' She got in and Richard followed her with the cases. The man took one of them from him, and they processed through the long empty corridor to her compartment.

The man took her ticket and said, 'There'll be a dining-car on at Glasgow.' She thanked him and he left them.

Richard said, 'I must go. They don't stop longer than they can help.'

'No,' she said. 'You go. I'll write from London.'

'Yes. You do that.' He was still kind and considerate and quite impersonal. She still did not know what he knew, or what he felt, or what he had it in mind to do. They had gone on with their arrangements for her move south exactly as if James had not died. He touched her lightly on the arm and left her. That was all he would ever have done in any case. They would no more have kissed in a train corridor than they would have made love on Brighton beach. He went off down the corridor. She heard the door slam, and almost at once the train started to move. She just saw him on the platform as the train went past him. They both raised a hand. Then she turned and shut the door of her compartment.

She stowed the big cases out of the way and opened the dressing case. She started to take out what she wanted. Her hand touched the stiff paper under her night things, and she pulled it out. Portrait of Catriona. She looked at it uncomprehendingly. It might have been someone she had known once, but not for very long. She tore it carefully in half, and then tore each half in half, and went on very deliberately until she had reduced it to fragments not much bigger than confetti, which she gathered carefully into a heap on the shiny surface of the flap table.

They were well away from Glenaidon now. The moor lay black and empty all round them, and already the bigger mountains were falling away to the northward. She did not want to see it, but she could hardly draw the blinds and put the lights on yet. There was a chamber-pot with a spout ingeniously built into the fixture under the wash basin. It had a warning notice saying it was not meant for solids, but this would hardly exclude confetti. She put a little water in the pot and scattered half a handful of the torn paper into it and sluiced it down the drain. Then she waited for another mile or so and sluiced down some more. By the time she was finished, the thing was scattered in tiny fragments over God knows how many miles of empty track in the middle of the wilderness, and it was starting to get dark. She drew the blinds then and turned on the lights.

She looked at herself in the glass, as she had when she had found herself alone on the journey up. She did not seem to look very different. She was back to the beginning now, exactly where she had been after Julia's death all those years ago. Then the numbness had come over her, but she could not remember very closely how long it had been before it came. She did not think it had been very long. It would come back again, she was sure of that. It was only a question of how long she had to wait.

www.ingramcontent.com/pod-product-compliance
Ingram Content Group UK Ltd.
Pitfield, Milton Keynes, MK11 3LW, UK
UKHW022312280225
455674UK00004B/269